CW00969800

The Lost Letters Of Cardinal Bessarion

For Julia

The Lost Letters Of Cardinal Bessarion

Matthew Stringer

© Matthew Stringer 2020

This book is a work of fiction.
Where real historical figures or past events are mentioned or alluded to their roles are entirely fictional.

ISBN 9798642402511

Contents

Figures

Falsa elephanti
fama refert vanis insomnia turbida portis,
somnia vera ferunt non vanae cornua famae.

(Basinio da Parma, *Hesperis* XIII 208-210)

Foreword

George Lewis Quain was, unfortunately, one of the early British casualties of the Covid-19 coronavirus pandemic, dying in February of this year. Permission having been granted by his executors, I have already published some of the literary oddities which were found in his library. These have included writings by one Dr. Alexander Blaikie Cromar dating to the early twentieth century. The documents contained herein conform to both those criteria, but are of a larger scope than the few poems appended to 'A Letter for Maggie Cromar'.

They are, once more, a product of Dr. Cromar's interests as an amateur antiquarian, this time concerning a collection of fifteenth century (*quattrocento*, in Dr. Cromar's idiom) letters which he apparently brought back from Italy in 1910. The letters themselves are not extant, nor do we have Dr. Cromar's full translations of them into English. Rather we have only Dr. Cromar's commentaries on them, or perhaps it would be more accurate to say his discussions of them. These include, it is true, significant translated excerpts from the letters, which in most cases indeed run to their full length, but otherwise we are left with a mere tantalising glimpse of what might have been available.

Accompanying Dr. Cromar's documents were found Quain's own notes thereon, which I have included as an appendix. These critique Dr. Cromar's work in more detail than I have competence for, and additionally provide further detail of Dr. Cromar. I shall limit myself here to noting that the presence of Dr. Cromar's documents in the library of George Lewis Quain owes nothing to Alexander's medical career, but instead to his amateur interests. These ranged broadly across archaeology, ancient and medieval history, classical literature, art history and, apparently, the Italian Renaissance.

It seems that these documents remained incomplete and unpublished at the time of Dr. Cromar's death, at the age of 69, in November 1919.

Also found within this collection of Dr. Cromar's papers were a series of related illustrations which I have distributed between the various written documents in an arrangement which seemed broadly appropriate.

Matthew Stringer

Aberdeen, May 2020

The Lost Letters Of Cardinal Bessarion

Introduction by Alexander Blaikie Cromar

During the spring of 1910 I was fortunate enough, upon my retirement from a career as a physician, to indulge my amateur passions with a journey to Italy and Greece: it was, in essence, my own Grand Tour.

I had initially travelled by rail to Venice, rather predictably. From there I continued to Ravenna, then down through the Malatesta territories of the Romagna, stopping in Rimini to see the *Tempio Malatestiano*, before reaching Ancona from where I crossed the Adriatic by steamer to Patras. Despite some misgivings about the political situation following the *coup d'état* of the previous year (which, as it happened, came to naught), in Greece I 'ticked off' a list of the key sites of antiquity following a clockwise pattern: Delphi, Thermopylae, Thebes, Athens, Epidauros, Mycenae, Sparta and Olympia. Returning to Ancona, I crossed Italy to Rome before turning north to Florence and Bologna.

It was there that I walked into a bookshop set in a shadowed backstreet off the *Via Zamboni*, central thoroughfare of that most venerable university district in all of Europe. The store, whose air was redolent with the particular chocolate-rich fragrance of old tomes, was arranged more akin to a grocer's than a library: the broad but shallow customer area beyond the door was barred from further ingress by a counter running the full width of the premises. Beyond this a wall of shelves crowded with volumes stretched to a high ceiling, punctuated at ground level by two open doorways through which I glimpsed that this labyrinth of literature extended backwards for some distance. I perceived the wisdom of this arrangement, given the conjunction of the rarity and value of the treasures for sale with the pressing want of the impecunious student *clientele*.

A junior member of staff attended to me initially, a youth with curly russet hair and a haughty demeanour which quite evaporated upon recognition of his ignorance of the answers to the questions posed by this northern foreigner. He became apologetically friendly, and called his grandfather through from the far recesses of the establishment to speak with me. That ancient gnome, not a foot taller than the counter, engaged me in conversation for several minutes before ushering me to the extreme end of the shop, where he opened a hatch and bid me cross the threshold to join him in the inner sanctum of his emporium.

It was over two hours later that I re-emerged into the day-lit world, bringing with me much treasure: a dozen volumes, of various ages (and prices) plus a folder in folio size of black card and red-marbled paper, bound with a leather thong. This held a collection of letters which, my host assured me - and my inspections indeed suggested - were several centuries old and of significant interest. I shall not, out of shame, divulge the financial cost of this shopping expedition. From Bologna I travelled to Milan and then home, via Lake Como, Switzerland and the Rhine.

I have, over the intervening years, made some inexpert translations of those letters which I brought from *Atti e Figli* of Bologna. This has required significant additional research in order to provide appropriate context, which has, in turn, led me to the belief that the collection represents a find of no little significance, revealing a conspiracy which, while largely of a piece with the accepted understanding of the political machinations of *quattrocento* Italy, has previously been lost to history.

Alexander Blaikie Cromar,

Aberdeen, 1919

Figure 3: The bookshop of *Atti e Figli*, Bologna, drawing by A.B. Cromar

The Letter of Poggio Bracciolini,

Chancellor of the Florentine Republic, to Cardinal Basilios Bessarion, July 1455

Of the twelve letters in this collection, the one dated as the earliest was written in the summer of 1455. As with the other eleven it was sent to one Cardinal Basilios Bessarion, who presumably kept them together as a set linked by some common theme. No copy of any letter by Bessarion (to which these would be replies) is included, nor, so far as I have yet been able to ascertain, is any extant elsewhere: these communications give every appearance of having been covert.

This letter was written in Latin. Its author, Gian Francesco 'Poggio' Bracciolini, was a scholar who had spent the larger part of his life working in the Papal court of the Vatican. The Latin he uses in this letter is not, though, that Ecclesiastical Latin which would have been the ordinary working language of the Church, but rather one in imitation of the Classical Latin of the later Roman Republic.

This is because Poggio was an early specimen of what is termed a humanist, and thus part of that intellectual movement which drove the cultural revolution which the esteemed Swiss, Jacob Burckhardt, has so volubly described in his work 'The Civilisation of the Renaissance in Italy'. While I sympathise with Burckhardt's antipathy towards reductive economic explanations of history of the Marxist kind, I hold not only that is it uncontentious to argue that the Renaissance had its birth in the city of Florence, but, moreover, that this can be traced to a single, key event without which, while the great current of history may have flowed in essentially the same direction, the particulars of its meanderings would have been quite different. It is not coincidental that Poggio, being an early humanist, was also a Florentine.

He was born not in the city itself, but in the dependent village of Terranuova, which has for the last half-century appended Bracciolini's name to its own in celebration of its famous son. Poggio's father took him to the city as a child to study under a *protégé* of Petrarch, whom we may regard as the Ur-humanist of the Florentines. Poggio trained as a legal notary, a profession which was in great demand in that most mercantile of cities: it had been the notional profession of Petrarch, although, as with Poggio, Petrarch was less interested in legal disputation for financial gain than in the intellectual world opened up to him by this education.

Petrarch - Francesco Petrarca - became fascinated by the writings of the ancient pagans, searching out forgotten manuscripts in monastic libraries across Europe. The oratory of Cicero became for him a particular model of a more elegant form of Latin than the debased usage of the contemporary church. He is credited with conceiving of the notion of the 'dark ages' stretching from the fall of Rome to his own day, and so, however embryonically, with an idea of the 'rebirth' of classical learning in his own time.

Humanism is so named because of its interest in the relations of humans to the things of the material world, in opposition to more spiritual or theological concerns. In addition to the knowledge of the classical world, it championed an interest in inquiry, in experiment and observation, of practical accomplishment and, therefore, in the worth of intellectual expression in languages other than the Ecclesiastical Latin of churchmen. Petrarch became one of the 'Three Crowns' of Florentine literature, along with Dante Alighieri and Giovanni Boccaccio, his most famous contribution being the development of the sonnet in the Florentine language: it is owed to these three that modern standard Italian descends, of all the varied languages of Italy of the *quattrocento*, from their native tongue. But their influence might not have spread beyond the borders of that Tuscan Republic were it not for the events of the year 1400.

It was then that the forces of Gian Galeazzo Visconti, Duke of Milan, laid siege to Florence in the course of an attempt to bring all northern Italy under Milanese dominion. At that time the Chancellor of Florence (that office occupied by Poggio Bracciolini when writing his letter to Cardinal Bessarion) was one Collucio Salutati, a humanist who had been a pupil of Petrarch. Collucio used his own humanist enthusiasm, by comparing the Florentine Republic to that of Classical Rome, to rouse the Florentines to successful resistance through this identification. In this way humanism became politically decisive at this specific place and time, accruing to itself a power it had previously lacked. Backed by Florentine mercantile wealth united against an external threat, a rebirth of classical culture exploded through the city. This political and economic success of Renaissance culture in Florence then caused it to spill out across northern Italy and, in time, all of Europe.

By 1455 Poggio Bracciolini had outlived his three score and ten allotted years. The *signoria* of the Florentine Republic had made him chancellor two years previously in recognition of his reputation. In contrast to Collucio Salutati, Poggio treated the position effectively as a sinecure, which was probably the spirit in which it was granted. He would survive four more years.

We do not know precisely to which questions of Bessarion's Poggio was responding, although indications may be gleaned from his reply. His letter is extremely long, wandering through and around many topics, being apparently the self-indulgent ramblings of an old man with, at last, the time to write whatsoever he pleased. I do not here provide a translation of the full document, but, rather, selected excerpts with such commentary as I regard as germane to the main question; that being, of course, Bessarion's underlying purpose which caused him to have collected together, and apparently hidden, the collection of letters of which this is the first.

Poggio begins his letter:

> Philosophy, the love of wisdom, is the laurel which has crowned the Hellene since the Seven Sages: I number Your Eminence in that illustrious company. Thank you for restraining Niccolò Perotti. I acknowledge my portion of blame in the matter, it being indeed regrettable that I said Messer Lorenzo might be better dealt with by the knife than the pen.

Poggio's coronation with classical laurel of the "Hellene" is an apparent compliment directed towards Bessarion, who had been a citizen of the Greek-speaking, 'Byzantine' eastern Roman Empire centred on Constantinople. The Seven Sages mentioned are Thales, Solon &c. of pre-classical Greek antiquity. Note, however, that his Latin is 'Philosophia, dilectio sapientiae': Poggio translates the Greek term into Latin although writing to a native speaker of Greek. This is presumably to emphasise its etymological origin for its practical application here, in opposition to the esoteric and arcane associations which had accrued to it, and which the word retains for us in English today.

It is additionally worth considering that the term "Hellene" had connotations of pre-Christian pagan Greek antiquity. It might be deemed a compliment from a humanist towards a Greek of similar inclinations, but Bessarion was a Cardinal of the Church. Additionally, he had previously been a priest of the Eastern Orthodox Church, having converted after his arrival in Italy. Is there a slight in respect of Bessarion's religious convictions contained within Poggio's apparent praise?

Two years prior to the date of this letter, the Niccolò Perotti mentioned by Poggio - author of the account of Ugo Tedeschini found amongst these letters - attempted to commission an assassin to kill Poggio. Niccolò had sided against Poggio in his public disagreement with a scholarly rival, Lorenzo Valla. At the time Perotti was teaching at the University of Bologna, while Bessarion was administering that city which fell within the purview of the Papal States. Bessarion succeeded in reining in his underling, a point which I discuss further in my commentary on Perotti's letter.

For Niccolò Perotti to have planned to have a man murdered over a difference of opinion regarding philology should strike us today as absurd. Note, however, Poggio's admission of the form of language used by the antagonists, which is typical of the time, even among men today elevated as scholars of surpassing genius. Their times are far from our own.

Poggio goes on to explain the source of his disagreement with Lorenzo: Valla had argued that techniques of philological analysis which he had developed for the study of ancient pagan texts could with equal validity be applied to scripture; Poggio's retort was that different species of truth required different treatments. He continues in conciliatory tone that he and Valla had put aside their differences, recognising that:

> Such must be the way for the fallible approaches of mortals to the understanding of creation and of God.

He goes on to say that the blame for his behaviour against Valla should in fact be placed upon one George Trapezuntius ('of Trebizond'). He explains:

> One day I overheard [George Trapezuntius] and recognised that he was making false accusations against me. Enraged, I approached him, declaring his mendacity to him and to his audience. Respecting neither my years nor my service to so many men in the seat of the Bishop of Rome, he struck me with his fist! There in the chancery of the Vatican court he

> knocked me to the floor, before simply retaking his seat. You may imagine my fury. I seized him by the face, in mind to force him to recognise his crime. At this he called for a sword! Of course he was thrown into the prison of the Castel Sant' Angelo for this outrage.

George of Trebizond was a scholar of Cretan origin, and a contributor of another of the letters in this collection. It is unique in not having been addressed to Bessarion, but was forwarded on to him by Pope Paul II. George is unlikely to have written to Bessarion, having taken umbrage against the Cardinal over Bessarion's criticism of a commentary George had written to accompany his translation of the *Almagest* of Ptolemy. This Greek text had recently become available to the Latin west and Pope Nicholas V had commissioned both a transliteration and a commentary of this work from Trapezuntius as a scholar with Greek as his native tongue. The linguistic skills of George Trapezuntius were undisputed, in contrast to those in mathematics and philosophy: while the translation was lauded, the commentary was not. Bessarion commissioned an alternative from the German scholars Georg von Peuerbach and Regiomontanus, to Trapezuntius' considerable *chagrin*.

The Castel Sant' Angelo mentioned is the mausoleum of Hadrian, across the *Pons Aelius* from Rome. It has only recently been decommissioned from its use as a fortress and a prison by the Vatican.

After his digression on the behaviour of Trapezuntius, Poggio continues:

> You indulge the vanity of an old man, Your Eminence, in suffering me to regale you with my reminiscences. By God's grace I still rest in the favour of Mnemosyne: my eyes discern each cypress upon the stark skyline, yet without my eyeglasses I can now read not a single word of the books written in my own fine and youthful hand; likewise, though recent days flow from my memory like water through careless fingers, the events of distant years stand sharp before the eye of my mind. I shall undertake to recount for you what I am able, as a layman, but one privileged with five decades of service to the *Curia,* of my recollections of the convolutions of the Latin Church in those remote days before we were blessed with your conversion.

Poggio finds, as is typical, that age has made both his memory (Mnemosyne, 'Memory', being mother of the Muses) and his sight long. His mention of the use of spectacles is not a trivial issue, for these had enabled scholars to continue to be able to read and write for far longer into old age than had previously been allowed by presbyopia. Developments in optics, both practical and theoretical, are a key technology associated with the period.

Poggio next expresses his condolences regarding the election in April 1455 of Alphonso da Borgia as Pope Callixtus III in preference to Bessarion himself. This followed the death of Pope Nicholas V who had been a great patron of scholarship, including humanist learning, providing plentiful work for men like Poggio Bracciolini, Lorenzo Valla and George of Trebizond. Alphonso da Borgia was, in Poggio's words:

> no lover of the humane arts, and burns with Valencian zeal for the re-conquest of Christian lands.

Poggio is here referring, in addition to the *Reconquista* ongoing in Iberia, to the fall of Constantinople to the Ottoman Turks in 1453 and Callixtus' desire to raise a western crusade for her recapture. Bessarion, though, as an exile from that fallen empire, would have been at least as motivated in this regard. Poggio, perhaps with more tact than conviction, proposes that the preference for Alphonso over Bessarion among their fellow cardinals lay in the recognition that, before the great schism between the western, Latin rite, Catholic Church and the eastern, Greek rite, Orthodox Church could be healed, first the schism within the western church itself must be mended, and that Alphonso represented the choice with more experience in that arena.

From here Poggio goes on to discuss, at some length, the history of the Papacy since the previous century: the divisions of Guelf and Ghibelline; the Avignon papacy; the convening of the Council of Constance by Sigismund King of the Germans to settle the issue; the election there of Martin V as the single Pope with the Vatican as his seat; the coronation of Sigismund as Holy Roman Emperor by Martin's successor, Pope Eugenius IV; and, amid this all, the Council of Basel and Florence.

This latter council was convened with the intent of healing the Great Schism and reconciling the churches of east and west: eastern hopes were for western military aid against the Turks; for the west the prize was recognition of the Bishop of Rome as Primate over all of Christendom. Originally established at Basel in 1431 by Pope Martin V under the terms agreed at the Council of Constance, Poggio has this to say:

> This was the Council to which the Emperor, the Patriarch, and others, yourself among them, were invited from Constantinople. Martin died, and his successor Eugene sent ships to Constantinople to bring the Emperor to a rival Council at Ferrara. It was at this Council - though perhaps, I think, when it had moved to Florence - that I first met you, Your Eminence, and also the lauded scholar of the Hellenes, Georgios Gemistus, called Pletho. I understand that he had been your teacher: I offer you my condolences, for I have heard that he died a few years ago in the Morea.

The move of the council to Ferrara was due to wrangling within the western church between Papal and Council factions; the subsequent move to Florence was a matter of Cosimo de' Medici providing more luxurious accommodation for the council in exchange for the prestige accrued to his native city, his family, and his person.

Poggio then mentions one Georgios Gemistus Pletho, who had indeed died in the Morea (as the Peloponnese was known at that time) in 1452, at an age of something over ninety years. Pletho was a famed Platonic scholar who had, as Poggio notes, educated Bessarion himself at Mystras, capital of the Morea. Pletho evidently made a significant impression on Poggio, who, having described Pletho's rational dismantling of the arguments of one Cardinal Cesarini, his sole contribution to the debate before the full council, goes on to say:

> It seemed to me that it was a matter of personal indifference to [Pletho] whether the Holy Spirit is held to proceed from the Father alone or from the Son also: his intervention appeared less motivated by theology than that he found the argument fatuous, and such a lack of intellectual rigour he would not abide.
>
> The other impression which I formed of Gemistus is of a similar lack of interest, but in a different matter: he did not appear to mind whether the union of the churches was achieved or not. While clearly aware that failure to achieve

> union would mean that no military aid for Constantinople would be forthcoming from the west, he evinced no concern whatsoever for the imminent Turkish threat. It has been my experience that men are generally moved by either worldly or spiritual concerns, but Pletho seemed to me motivated by neither, being interested in reason alone. I understood why he was regarded as a very great philosopher.

There is a connection between Pletho and another person mentioned in Poggio's circumlocutions, the relevance of which will become apparent in several other letters of this collection. In his discussion of the Council of Constance, Poggio mentions of Pope Gregory XII:

> Gregory, old and infirm, lodged in Rimini. He was hosted there by Carlo Malatesta who came as legate to announce Gregory's abdication. It happens that my family has cause for gratitude to this Carlo Malatesta, for my father found refuge under his protection from some who made claims as creditors against him. My own first work as a notary, before quitting Florence, was to draft a letter of recommendation for my father's return. Carlo, though a *condottiere*, was a servant of the Church, unlike his nephew Sigismondo who now rules in Rimini: I have recently dedicated my work 'On the Misery of the Human Condition' to that man, who was last year excluded from the Peace of Lodi for his treachery to Naples. I think he will surely bring disaster on himself, and perhaps on all Italy, through his pride and presumption.

We will read a lot more of this *condottiere* (the term denotes a mercenary commander of the constant warfare which beset *quattrocento* Italy) Sigismondo Malatesta of Rimini throughout these letters. It may not be too much to claim that this passing mention of Sigismondo holds the key which may unlock the whole mystery of the collection and the secrecy with which Bessarion guarded it.

There is another particularly noteworthy digression made by Poggio dating to the Council of Constance. At this time, the Council having judged John XXIII an antipope, Poggio found himself without employment, and so, in imitation of Petrarch, he had travelled to various monasteries of the Germans to seek out forgotten manuscript copies of ancient authors in their libraries. His journey was very significant, especially at the monastery of the Benedictines at Fulda, in the Landgraviate of Hesse, where:

> as for Ulysses and Aeneas and Dante before me, I happened upon a host of the shades of the dead: Tertullian; Silius Italicus with his *Punica;* the *Astronomica* of Manilius and *Res Gestae* of Amminius Marcellinus, although missing, I estimate, almost the first half; grammars and critiques, and then, most singular of all, a codex with that work of Titus Lucretius Carus which has gained no little infamy in the intervening years, *De rerum natura.* Of course the doctrine is reprehensible. As a piece of poetry, however, as a vision of the Latin language as it should be used, as the exemplar not of the truth of an argument but of the style of argumentation, I consider it without peer, save only, perhaps, Virgil.

We may, I think, safely assume that in this portion of his account Poggio is indulging his own passions rather than in any sense responding to a query made by Bessarion. He places his rediscovery of texts in the literary tradition of visiting the underworld and speaking to the ghosts of the dead. It is possible that Poggio Bracciolini felt that he was indeed allowing the voices of the illustrious dead to be heard above the earth once more, for his journey would have been a matter of no small discomfort, inconvenience, and danger, and so his devotion to his task was not inconsiderable.

Lucretius' 'On Nature', composed during the turmoil of the late Roman Republic, expounded the doctrine of Epicureanism in Latin poetry of a quality admired a generation later by Horace, Ovid and Virgil, who Poggio deems Lucretius' only peer. Poggio was wise to disavow Lucretius' message, however: by the time of his letter to Bessarion, that poem and its creed of Epicureanism had become synonymous with atheism. It will be observed, in the first letter written by Nicholas of Cusa in this collection, that the accusation of Epicureanism was among those made by Pope Pius II against Sigismondo Malatesta.

The retrieval of Lucretius' infamous poem by Poggio Bracciolini is, however, already known from other sources, while the same does not apply to an interesting and suggestive episode from his homeward journey:

> For my return I made for Mainz, intending thence to follow the Rhine southward. Having been provided with a letter of

> recommendation to the Bishop, in that city was extended to me the hospitality of a merchant of that town whose name escapes me now. Dining that evening in the family home, a son who was apprenticed as a goldsmith showed a great interest in my quest. He asked me to demonstrate my famous handwriting for him, questioned me at length about the aesthetics of presenting a book, and asked to see the copied texts which were in my possession. He had little Latin, and I no German, but my man translated between us adequately enough. I have since heard that Aeneas Piccolomini has, this very year, seen in Hesse a bible not written by the hand of man, but created instead by a contrivance derived from the wine-press. Of course I cannot know, but I suspect its inventor to be none other than that lad; might it be that I lit in him the spark which will kindle and burn to ashes my whole craft?

It may seem to invoke coincidence to a preposterous degree to suggest that Poggio Bracciolini inspired Johannes Gutenberg to the invention of printing with moveable type. But it is perhaps not as far-fetched as all that, unless one is prepared to suggest Gutenberg's inspiration was *ex nihilo*: for something inspired the young Gutenberg to mechanise the copying of books, to see if he could, through his metalworking skills, bypass the years of practice and effort Poggio Bracciolini had poured into perfecting his cursive script, his hands aching with arthritis at every stroke of the pen.

The report of Aeneas Piccolomini (who in 1458 became Pope Pius II) encountering Gutenberg's bible is known from a letter dated to the 12th of March 1455, sent by Piccolomini to his employer at that time, Cardinal Juan de Carvajal. This was a mere dozen days before the death of Pope Nicholas V which precipitated the conclave (attended by Carvajal) where Alphonso da Borgia was elected in preference to Bessarion. Piccolomini's letter was almost lost to scholarship. The observation may be made that the world of Renaissance political and intellectual life was small by modern standards, and paths did cross and intertwine more often than we might naïvely expect.

In any event what is true is that these letters were written at the end of the manuscript age: while Poggio Bracciolini represented, as a humanist, a waxing cultural current, he was also towards the end of a scribal tradition, of men who made a living through their handwriting, which dated back millennia to the birth of writing. By the time of the death of Basilios Bessarion in 1472 there were printing presses using Gutenberg's moveable type in all the major cities of Italy - indeed Bessarion was a sponsor of the first in Rome - and by the end of the century more than twenty million volumes had been printed in Western Europe. It was a revolution in communications, which would, as Poggio foresaw, "kindle and burn to ashes [his] whole craft." Only the rise of modern wireless radiotelegraphy in recent years has offered any significant alternative to print for the purposes of mass communication.

I give the final, somewhat disconsolate section of Poggio's letter without further comment:

> I have devoted five full decades of my life to service in the Papal *Curia*, since the days of Boniface (IX). I have served seven different men as pontiff, most recently of course Nicholas. The weariness I came to feel for the work was never on account of the requests of Holy Father Nicholas, in whom we were blessed with a man of supreme humanist learning and taste. Some few years ago I dedicated 'On the Inconstancy of Fortune' to him. In it I recalled a walk around the ancient ruins of Rome in the company of Antonio Loschi, something we had done many times before. We sat in an archway, an orphaned remnant of some Tarpeian temple looking out over the wasteland that had been the Forum, and recalled with irony Virgil's celebration "now golden, once wild with tangled bushes" (Virgil, *Aeneid* 8.348) and we mourned that time and chance had reversed the scene as precisely as if reflected in a temporal mirror, returning all that celebrated glory to the briars and brambles of the wild. It is not forgotten though; for not only may we still read the words of Virgil and all those other illustrious men of old rescued from the ignominy of the dungeons such as at Saint Gall and Fulda, but they may still inspire us to equal them today.
>
> I offer to you my personal commiserations on the fall of Constantinople to the Turks, having had no previous opportunity so to do. This is a great and dark event for all Christendom; yet now that we have unity within our Church,

inspired by that passionate devotion to the faith which Holy Father Callixtus brings from Spain, we may hope that the heresies and divisions of Latin Christendom are behind us forever. Perhaps we may even dare to hope that we will see the end of schism between the Churches of east and west, so that not only Constantinople, but Christianity across the world might be defended from those who deny Christ's truth.

I shall desist from subjecting you further to the tedium of an old man's recollections of the tribulations of former years. For my part, I have valued freedom all my life, and ever maintained my mind free as its own place: I now possess in addition some leisure, for whatever time Providence might still assign to me, though the times in which we now live bring their own travails.

Figure 4: The Roman forum imagined as the overgrown wasteland seen by Poggio Bracciolini, drawing by A.B. Cromar

The Letter of Thomas Palaiologos,

Heir to the Imperial Throne of Constantinople, to Cardinal Basilios Bessarion. September 1460.

This second letter is from one of the younger brothers of Constantine XI Palaiologos, the last Byzantine Emperor, who had died in battle in May 1453 when Constantinople fell to the Turks.

Thomas Palaiologos had ruled the Despotate of the Morea - the rump Byzantine polity in the Peloponnese - in partnership with his older brother Demetrios until its annexation in 1460 by Sultan Mehmet II. Thomas fled to Rome under Cardinal Bessarion's sponsorship where he was hailed as rightful claimant to the throne of Constantinople, Demetrios having chosen to kowtow to the Sublime Porte.

The letter being short, I provide below a full translation from the original Greek, albeit interspersed with my commentary notes:

> And so, dear Basilios, I come to you, to the west, the sun having set on the Morea. Forgive me that I am ignorant of the etiquette proper to your rank as a Cardinal of the Latin Church. I come as a poor man, an outcast seeking refuge, one quite lost but for your Christian charity, having nothing in the world of value with which to pay his way. I carry in my veins the blood of Emperors, but with no empire what is that?
>
> You have ever given faithful service to my house, as you now extend your hand in aid. My wife and our children I shall leave at Corfu, in the fortress of Angelokastro. They are in the care of the Venetians, who are her people. I myself shall come to Rome, as you advise. I shall be guided by you, Father. You have made all arrangements for our safety to date with your characteristic thorough competence. I shall perform for the Princes of Italy like a tame Syrian bear, teeth pulled, claws clipped. I shall dance for scraps in the court of the Bishop of Rome, that our city, our lands and our people may one day be free of the Sultan's yoke.

In respect of Thomas' claim of ignorance with regard to the correct form of address for Bessarion's position, it is quite implausible that such a point of etiquette should be beyond a member of the Imperial family: here we must assume him to be making an oblique expression of distaste for Bessarion's conversion to the Latin church.

The wife whom Thomas reports leaving on Corfu was Catherine Zaccaria, daughter of Centurione II Zaccaria of the Principality of Achaea. This had been the final vestige of the Latin Empire, by which is meant the feudal Crusader state established over much of the Byzantine territories following the shameful sack of Constantinope in 1204 by the Fourth Crusade. Thomas' ancestor, Michael VIII Palaiologos, had restored the Empire of the Byzantines in 1261, and by the early fifteenth century the Latins had been driven to the western margins of the Peloponnese. In 1430 Constantine and Thomas Palaiologos had taken that too, whereupon Centurione married his daughter to Thomas and lived out his life in his castle at Messina. In common with many of the islands of both the Ionian and Aegean seas, Corfu was in the possession of the Venetians, and strong fortresses such as that of Angelokastro mentioned by Thomas ensured that the island never fell to the Turks.

Thomas continues:

> It will be good to see you, and to have one friend among the strangers of the foreign land. I wonder if our eyes will know each other after all the years since we last met? I believe it was in Mystras at the funeral of the wife of Theodore my brother, Cleofa of the house of Malatesta. Do you know that twenty-seven years have passed since that day? The old scholar Gemistus read the main oration, but you, as I recall, delivered also a poem in fine iambics. Cleofa was not old when she died, but then we were all young at that time, excepting of course Gemistus. He had the air of a Methuselah living out so many years until finally he died as the Ottoman flood rose to engulf Constantinople.

Mystras clings to the eastern face of Mount Taygetos from where it looks across the Eurotas' vale to the unprepossessing ruins of Sparta. The Byzantine town is crowned with a high fortress built by Guillaume de Villehardouin, Frankish Prince of Achaea, following the establishment of the Latin Empire.

Cleofa Malatesta (c. 1403 - 1433) was daughter to Malatesta dei Sonnetti of Pesaro, second cousin of Sigismondo Malatesta. Though the branches of the family were belligerent to one another, the source of the connection to the Morea and ancient Laconia felt by Sigismondo is here demonstrated.

From this point Thomas' letter becomes, in effect, an elegy for Constantinople:

> Ah, Father Bessarion, how great must be our Christian sins that God should treat us so! And yet I know some of them, and very terrible those sins to be. For our city's great and ancient walls, which had stood since the Younger Theodosius was Emperor, fell not to the trumpets of the Lord and the presence of the Ark, but to a monstrous bombard beyond the skill of the Turks to cast. This was made by a Magyar smith in treachery to his native land and Christian faith, for mere gold. It is said that he was killed as the walls finally fell, in an explosion of his terrible gun. Perhaps he has discovered that the Catholics are indeed correct that Hell is a real place, and he now waits out eternity with Iscariot and the other traitors.

Thomas compares the fall of Constantinople to the Biblical account of the fall of the walls of Jericho (*Joshua* 6:1-21). The Hungarian gunsmith Thomas mentions, who was named Orban, had initially offered his skills to Emperor Constantine. When he found that beleaguered Constantinople was by this time too impecunious to afford his services, he promptly went over to the Sultan.

Thomas' implication of a clear distinction between the dogmas of Latin and Greek churches in respect of the issue of the reality of Hell is questionable, although in the western popular view it was certainly portrayed as a matter of geography, notably in the 'Divine Comedy' of Dante.

> Accounts have come to us from some few who survived the fall, and fled, and came to Mystras. They tell of slaughter and pillage, the destruction of so much that was venerable, especially of the churches. The Muslims, iconoclasts, went through all the lesser churches of the city and destroyed every image of Christ, every sacred icon of the Virgin and every saint, every cross. They reached the ancient centre, the site of the hippodrome, and the Shrine of the Holy Wisdom of God. The people had fled there, huddled in their

> hundreds, and barred the doors. These the Turks stormed and broke, and rushed into that holy place even as the priests there holding Mass walked out through solid walls. Rape and murder were done in the sight of God, and the people taken away to be slaves. Then Sultan Mehmed came and decreed the place a mosque, bidding them call their alien prayers from the pulpit, and set men to tearing down all the mosaics, raising up in their place banners bearing the name of God in their serpentine script.
>
> I recall staring up to that ceiling as a young child: by day with shafts of sunlight crossing silently from windows far above, as between parting clouds, lighting the lofty vaults to golden heaven beneath the vast blue dome floating serene above it all; or at night when a thousand candles shone back flickering from myriad myriad gold and silver *tessarae* embedded in the deep indigo of that majestic canopy. That it had hung there for over nine centuries was, for me, the Empire; not the might of armies, the wealth of trade, the walls, the castles, the palaces, or even the multitudes and generations who had lived out their lives within its refuge. Simply, but magnificently, this greatest roof in all the world, this earthly assemblage of mere stone contrived as a reflection of heaven, demonstrated to me that our polity was ordered not by man but by God's will. And they have destroyed it. It is gone. Ah, the high-blown pride of ancestors born in the purple, humbled, brought to nothing after all.

Thomas here gives the full name customarily abbreviated as *Hagia Sophia*, Holy Wisdom. He recounts the legend that those priests who were celebrating Mass walked into the walls, there to await the reconsecration of the great church, at which time they will return.

Thomas epitomises his grief for the fall of the city and the empire through the synecdoche of the dome of *Hagia Sophia*. This crowned the commission of Justinian the Great, succeeding the dome of the Pantheon in Rome as the world's largest. Its span exceeds that of the dome of the Cathedral of Florence, completed in 1436, some nine centuries later, by Filippo Brunelleschi: it should, however, be noted that Brunelleschi's construction eliminates the need for the heavy buttressing of *Hagia Sophia*.

The band of high windows encircling the base of the *Hagia Sophia* dome provide the effects of light here described by Thomas, while also serving to reduce the supported mass. Although everything on which the eye falls within that colossal interior is stone, Roman practise required that all surfaces were decorated. In this case this is achieved with Byzantine mosaic: it is modelled, plastic art, the earthly substances of which it is formed irrelevant to its representation of heaven. I have given 'myriad myriad' for the numbering of these *tesserae* of mosaic where the Greek has feminine genitives *myriados myriadōn*, thus specifically "from ten thousand ten thousands". This number being no exaggeration of the count of *tesserae* which would have decorated the great church, the effect is more arresting than an unspecified 'innumerable'.

The royal associations of purple were of venerable antiquity, the Canaanites of the Levant coast having been given by the Greeks the name 'Phoenician' for their use of the murex sea-snail to manufacture of the opulent clothing-dye known as 'Tyrian purple'. At Constantinople in the Great Palace a free-standing pavilion was built, of solid plagioclase porphyry, that imperial children might be literally 'born in the purple'.

> And so I shall not steer my ship of life against the tide, but follow Fortune's tack and come to Italy, where sweet life shall ebb away as I look out over the unresting sea, and shed tears. I confess to little faith that we shall win succour for Constantinople. I come with empty hands, having no gifts to bring. But I think, Father Bessarion, that they fear us, even when we bear no gifts.

Thomas ends with two classical references. The first is taken from book 5 of the *Odyssey* of Homer, where Odysseus, stranded on the island of Ogygia, yearns for home. The second is from the second book of Virgil's *Aeneid*, a Latin work, presumably to demonstrate his familiarity with the literary traditions of the west to Bessarion: he paraphrases the Trojan priest Laocoön's warning in respect of the wooden horse: "I fear Greeks, even when they bear gifts".

This short letter, elegiac though it may be, cannot hope to convey the magnitude of psychic catastrophe felt by Thomas and other Byzantines at the fall of Constantinople. This was the New Rome of Constantine, the Emperor whose conversion had assured Christianity's standing in this world. Her sack by fellow Christians in the Fourth Crusade had been an outrage, with slaughter and destruction which was, if anything, worse than that perpetrated by the Ottomans; but for the Holy City to fall into Muslim hands was incomprehensible. Even in Rome, where the shame of the failure of the Crusades to retain Jerusalem under Christian rule was felt as a challenge to Papal claims of ultimate divine authority on earth, the loss of Constantinople was a profound blow. Something would have to be done.

Figure 5: The Magyar smith Orban With his gun, drawing by A.B. Cromar

The Letter of Niccolò Perotti,

to Cardinal Bessarion, May 1461

This letter of Niccolò Perotti is unique within the collection in that it purports to be the account of a person not otherwise historically attested. This is not Perotti himself, who had been Secretary to Bessarion some fifteen years previously, as mentioned by Poggio Bracciolini in his letter in regard to his disagreement with Lorenzo Valla: indeed, by the date at which this letter was written Perotti was a bishop in his own right. Rather it appears that Perotti sent to Bessarion an account of Sigismondo Malatesta by an ordinary soldier who had fought in his service, one Ugo Tedeschini.

This presumably followed from Perotti's familiarity with Malatesta lands and the Romagnol tongue: Niccolò was native to Sassoferrato in the Marches, territory of the Malatesta of Pesaro. We may assume that this letter transcribes an interview by Perotti of Tedeschini, perhaps at Tedeschini's home in Balduccia, after a request by Bessarion for testimony regarding Sigismondo Malatesta. The original was written in Ecclesiastical Latin.

Due to its special interest I provide a translation of the full text of Perotti's letter, albeit interspersed with some commentary as necessary. Perotti commences thus:

> Being the testament of Ugo Tedeschini of Balduccia in respect of his service to Sigismondo Pandolfo Malatesta Lord of Rimini, as recorded by Niccolò Perotti.
>
> My father Pietro Tedeschini was a prosperous farmer of wheat and pigs and olives at Balduccia, on the right bank of the Marecchia a few miles upstream of Rimini. My mother Maria was the only daughter of Matteo dei Papielli, who had travelled from town to town and court to court with a troupe of players, and so knew many stories. As a young boy my brothers and sisters and I heard these tales while sat at his knee, for he came to live with us in his dotage. I loved most of all the French tales of valiant knights and fair ladies, brave deeds and pure hearts; of Roland, Yvain, Perceval, of the search for the Grail.

It happened that one festival day in Rimini a joust was held by our prince, Carlo Malatesta, and Matteo took me to watch. Amid the fluttering pennants, gleaming armour, shields of bright-hued devices, the snorting, thundering chargers and the clash of arms, all my grandfather's stories were made real before my eyes. Within the year I apprenticed as a page to my master Pietro Minardi, a lancer in Carlo's personal retinue.

After five years I was made squire to Pietro when Carlo knighted him after the battle at Motta, where Giovanni was killed who had been Pietro's squire before. We had been hard pressed by the forces sent from King Sigismund of Hungary, with many slain and Carlo himself hurt so sorely that he had to cede command to his brother Pandolfo, coming to our aid from Fano with a thousand lances. Three years later we met that same King Sigismund in peace when he called together the Council of the Church in Constance: Carlo attended as the Legate of Holy Father Gregory, who himself stayed in Rimini as Carlo's guest. In Constance I saw the Bohemian Jan Hus burned for preaching the heretical doctrines of the Englishman John Wycliffe. I am not a learned man, Your Reverence, and I hate Hell, but I confess that to me it seemed that this scholar died more bravely than do many men under arms. Such are the Devil's tricks.

Over the following years my master and I served Prince Carlo in all his campaigns until Sir Pietro was killed at Zagonara. That was when we fought for Florence, to relieve the siege of the castle there by the Milanese of Duke Filippo Visconti. Prince Carlo and some thousands more were taken captive. I was among the few who escaped to Cesena with lord Pandolfo, who raised me to a man-at-arms as a lancer. I remained in his service until Carlo was ransomed from Duke Filippo.

It was three years later that Pandolfo Malatesta died and his bastard sons, Galeotto Roberto, Gismondo and Domenico, came into the care of Carlo and his wife Elizabetta, who was of the house of Gonzaga of Mantua and a woman of utmost Christian piety. Carlo himself died only two years later, and rule of Rimini passed to Galeotto Roberto.

> This Galeotto was, like his aunt, a pious Christian, but ill-suited to rule, and no soldier. And so it was that forces immediately moved against him, which would not have been dared with Carlo alive. Holy Father Martin urged the Malatesta of Pesaro, led by the son of Malatesta dei Sonnetti, to seize Rimini, aided by Guidantonio da Montefeltro from Urbino.

This passage provides several dateable events. The Battle of Motta occurred in 1412. Assuming for Tedeschini an age of seven at the time of his apprenticeship as page, and accounting for the intervening five years mentioned until this battle, we may infer for Ugo a date of birth in the year 1400. The Battle of Zagonara was in 1424. Pandolfo Malatesta died in 1427, his brother Carlo in 1429. Of Pandolfo's three sons, Galeotto Roberto was born in 1411 to Allegra de' Mori, while Gismondo and Domenico were both sons of Antonia da Barignano, born 1417 and 1418 respectively. Martin here is, of course, Pope Martin V. Malatesta dei Sonnetti ('of the Sonnets' for his love of the form) was father to Cleofa Malatesta named in the letter of Thomas Palaiologos, and second cousin to Sigismondo Malatesta. Guidantonio da Montefeltro was father to Sigismondo's great *condottiere* rival Federico da Montefeltro of Urbino, a bastard whom Guidantonio had legitimised.

> Galeotto did not stir in his own defence: he deemed this action, being after all ordered by the Holy Father, to be the will of God. His brother Gismondo was much different in character, and although in but his fourteenth year, he called the men of Rimini to arms and led us out by night to fall upon the encamped enemy and disperse them. The Holy Father recognised Galeotto's rule after this, but the lords of Pesaro and Urbino were not content. When presently Galeotto died leaving no heir, rule of Rimini passed to Gismondo, although the wives of Carlo and Galeotto held the regency due to his youth. One Andrea della Serra, supported by Pesaro and Urbino, invaded the land and besieged Rimini, and might have taken it but that Gismondo took at once a horse and rode out from the town through the encircling forces, returning presently at the head of some thousands of the people brought from Cesena, whom he led against the enemy. Seeing this, we in the town sallied,

catching the forces of della Serra between two fronts. They fled, and the field was ours. After this Gismondo assumed rule in his own right, but then split the realm with his younger brother. Domenico was to rule north of the Rubicon, from Cesena, while the southern part, bordering the lands both of Pesaro and also Urbino, stayed with Gismondo who ruled from Rimini. The new Holy Father (Pope Eugenius IV) recognised their claims.

It was not long after these events that King Sigismund was crowned Emperor by the Holy Father in Rome. On his return Sigismund stopped in Rimini, where Gismondo gave him hospitality with all his retinue; and with Domenico, too, come from Cesena to accompany them northward. The Emperor had heard of this wondrous child Gismondo Malatesta, martial and valiant, not yet seventeen, and knighted both him and Domenico. They were the first to be knighted by a Holy Roman Emperor for many, many years, since Sigismund's father was alive. Sigismund being that same monarch who had inaugurated the Order of the Dragon for Christendom's defence, but now Emperor, crowned so by an undisputed Pope in Rome, this was a great honour for two orphans born as bastards, and both boys took new names for themselves from that time. Gismondo added to his name the sigil "SI" with which he has since decorated the Church of Saint Francis in Rimini, and became Sigismondo after the Emperor, adopting as his patron Saint Sigismund the Burgundian. Domenico became known simply as Malatesta Novello. I do not know why both the brothers wished to cast off the names they had worn as children, but both from that time on assumed their full selves.

So reconciled was Sigismondo with Pope Eugenius after this that two years later he was provided with Papal expenses for the maintenance of a troop of two hundred lances, six hundred mounted men in all, for the defence of his territories as a vicar of the Papal States. Those few of us whom he retained at his own expense as the lord of Rimini were also with him, and he was starting to make a name as a *condottiere*. At that time the two greatest captains in Italy were

Francesco Sforza and Niccolò Piccinino; Sigismondo sought to learn from them both, though he served mostly under Sforza. But Sigismondo had also his own native cunning, as I shall illustrate from an encounter in the early spring of those his younger years.

Sforza had fought for Milan until, having taken Ancona, he appealed to the Holy Father, changed sides in the conflict, and was granted the title of vicar of the city. Following this, when Sforza was besieging Assisi on the orders of the Pope, Francesco the son of Piccinino was moving southwards from Venetian territory towards Tuscany to join his father who intended then to engage Sforza. Francesco Piccinino's strength was around four thousand horse and six thousand foot, and they came into the Papal territories west of Cesena. Sigismondo joined with Novello his brother and moved to intercept them. Our strength was around two thousand horse and four thousand foot between the brothers, the infantry being mostly a militia of the local people to resist the despoiling of their land.

We brought our forces a league west from Cesena along the Via Emilia, with Piccinino still north of us, and made our camp around a knoll off to the south of the road where they would doubtless know of us by outrider report. They crossed the road also, between us and Cesena, and set their camp in the plain beneath ours, on the opposite side of one of the rivers which flows north from the hills out across the plain of the Po; I believe it to be named the Savio. This river was in spate, its waters icy, and a light snow lay over the dead ground. With nightfall we could see the many fires of their larger camp from the vantage of our own.

On our side of the river two small streams flowed eastward down to it, one north of the rise of our camp, the other south. The courses of both were choked thick with tangled scrub and low trees. Sigismondo summoned we who formed his permanent troop and divided our number in two, commanding us to hide ourselves in the undergrowth of these two waterways under the cover of darkness, our horses left in the rear of our camp. We did so, I in the contingent allotted the northern stream, and spent the long night with little sleep as the cold sank deeper and deeper into our bones, watching with envy the glow of fires from both camps through the foliage of our concealment.

As dawn first gleamed through the hazy mist which sat across the frozen ground, we heard the rumble of massed cavalry off to our right, from our own camp; and then directly before us, along the hedges within which we shivered, thundered hundreds of lancers. Beyond the flickering legs I made out a similar number on the far side of the plain before the barrier of that other stream's knotty underbrush.

The riders plunged on into the icy river, slowed as the horses struggled against the cold, and then melted into the mist which concealed the enemy camp. Alarms sounded, and the clash of arms, and then there they were, returning, crashing through the cold current and on up banks already churned to mud by their previous pass. They lumbered up and rode off before us, splitting around the two sides of the high ground of our camp on which our infantry, we now saw, were formed up.

Scarcely were the last of our lancers past us than the first of the enemy came on, likewise spurring their reticent mounts through the wintery waters, likewise labouring up the muddy banks. They came in large numbers stretched all across the field before us, but on reaching our bank some rode on, while some hesitated, looking to form up before advancing, and so their strength was drawn out across the plain.

Then came their infantry, a great mass of pikemen churning through the river. We had thought ourselves cold where we were, huddled under thick greenery, wriggling stiff toes and fingers to keep them from freezing to immobility, but saw and understood the icy chill soaking through Piccinino's men as they waded chest-deep through that bitter spate. As horses circled before them, they struggled slowly up the bank, as though broken by age, before forming up and coming slowly on across the open ground towards our camp; our infantry likewise advanced down to meet them.

Once Piccinino's infantrymen were past halfway from the river to our camp, our lancers rode back down either flank in dense formation, engaging not the pikemen but their disarrayed horsemen, cutting them down or routing them. At this we broke cover, as instructed, those nearest the river first, and then steadily more and more along the courses of either stream, at the run, across the rear of their infantry. They knew nothing of us, pressing on our main body of infantrymen ahead of them, hemmed in on either flank by cavalry, still moving with ponderous stiffness from their river crossing. And so we, though few in number and unaccustomed to using our lances on foot, found easy prey in these practiced pikemen. Some of our cavalry circled around to our rear in case of a counter-charge by their lancers, but it never came. We pressed their infantry and the greater number of them simply dropped their weapons and fell into the mud before us, begging mercy. Some in their centre formed a square, and broke forwards through our lines, being seasoned mercenaries, unlike the citizens of Cesena and its hinterland who made up the greater part of our infantry. This unit then retreated northwest from the field in good order, but most of the rest we took prisoner and ransomed.

Over the next several years war was continuous across all the north of Italy, although minor for the most part. Francesco Sforza, Niccolò Piccinino, Taddeo d'Este, Niccolò Fortebraccio, Federico da Montefeltro, Sigismondo Malatesta and more vied both for *condotte* and on the field of battle. Sigismondo was not always victorious, but he won more often than one might expect from simple consideration of the forces available to him; for when these were inadequate, he was, as in the example just recounted, cunning rather than foolhardy.

Another noteworthy episode occurred some few years later. Having faced greater numbers once again, we were driven from the field. I myself was among a group of lancers who charged through the enemy line, but then saw that our cause was lost and rode for our native territory. We thought to hear that our captain was dead, for he had crashed into the

> heart of the enemy's strength, and by his shield's device they knew him. Yet he returned to Rimini only two days after I did, in the company of two mere pikemen, without horse or armour, but all unblemished.
>
> His companions told how they had been returning along one of the roads through the hills when a wanderer wrapped in a poor cloak, mere sackcloth, alone and unarmed, met them as they drank at a stream. They walked with him; that evening they came to a village where one of them had kin with whom they would stay, and they asked him to join them. Brought into the kinsman's hut, they were all three welcomed to his humble table. The fare was *farinata* and a stew of garbanzo beans, but for men who had not eaten for two days it seemed as though the board groaned beneath a feast's weight. They asked the stranger to do them the honour of a grace, and as he spoke, and broke the bread, his cloak fell from him and they saw beneath it all his princely finery, and they knew him for their lord. Laughing, he bid his soldiers and their good host join him in their honest fare of chickpeas. I know all those who shared that meal with him to have thereafter been well rewarded.

The allusion in Perotti's Latin here to the Gospels of Luke (24:13-35) and Mark (16:12-13), comparing Sigismondo Malatesta to the risen Christ, is unmistakable. Were the comparison present in the account given to him by Ugo Tedeschini, Perotti would surely have noted it: it can, therefore, only reasonably be his own interpolation. His purpose is of course wholly opaque.

Is there additionally a reference to Cicero in specifying food consisting in chickpeas: '*ciceri*'? It may be pertinent here to note that Perotti had an interest in fables, it being from he that we have the beast tales of Aesop translated into Latin in a manuscript discovered in the Vatican library in 1831, presumably originally at the behest of Pope Nicholas V.

> It was only months later that Sigismondo, having amassed sufficient funds, commenced building his fortress in Rimini, the Castel Sismondo. The Malatesta have many strong castles in their lands, being skilled in their construction: this was such, built to withstand siege and the largest and newest guns. Its construction took many years; before it was fully

> finished, but when the main halls of his residence were adequately complete, Sigismondo announced a masque was to be held there in celebration. I was by this time held in sufficient esteem to be invited, and so attended.
>
> The great hall was noble, fit for the court of the Prince, with a high roof of carved timbers, a floor of fine coloured marble and the walls all hung and mounted with works of tapestry and fresco and carving in relief. Two particularly I recall: the first was a tapestry of a man in shining armour who looked up to a golden chalice mounted above in blood-red samite, and around it great angels, awful shapes, and wings and eyes. His shield bore a device of golden lions on an azure ground, and I knew him for Lancelot of the Lake glimpsing the Grail, the most valiant of those chivalrous knights from the old poems of France which I had loved so well as a child. The second work, in bright tempera, I thought at first might be a scene from the *Commedia* of Dante the Florentine: for it showed two men, one older, hooded as I had seen the shade of the poet Virgil portrayed, who, from among the stars and spheres of heaven, showed to his companion the earth below them and some great city. I saw, though, that the younger man was not the poet of the Florentines, but some warrior of the old pagans. Basinio da Parma was there, a man of much learning of the ancients who became a poet of Sigismondo's court: I asked him of it, and he recounted to me in a high style that these were the Scipios, ancestors of Sigismondo and the House of Malatesta, the scene taken from the dream recounted by Marcus Tullius Cicero: the dream belongs to the younger Scipio, shortly before he was to sack the city of Carthage which had vied with Rome.

Basinio of Parma was the composer of the *Hesperis*, an epic in praise of Sigismondo, and perhaps the finest Latin poet in the Italy of his day. Book 6 of the *Republic* of Cicero, commonly referred to as 'The Dream of Scipio' is the source to which Basinio is referring here. Note that in the two images we contrast the greatest of Christian knights and sacred quests with Cicero's legend of the greatest soldiers of the Roman Republic. There is also the question of whether this further reference to Cicero has allusory relevance given the earlier note regarding '*ciceri*'.

> I inquired further, for I, who knew so well those French tales of Christian knights, knew also so very little of our pagan but glorious Italian forebears. Basinio indulged me. He told me of the older Scipio, whose shade guided his grandson in the scene we looked upon, who was known as Africanus for defeating that great duke of Carthage, Hannibal son of Hamilcar, who had ravaged Italy and threatened even Rome with destruction. He told me of their great battles, at the Trebbia, at Trasimene, and at Cannae. It was as I questioned Basinio that I recognised that Sigismondo's stratagem against Francesco Piccinino at the Savio, of which I spoke earlier, was a very mirror of that of Hannibal at the Trebbia, merely on a smaller scale and moved farther down the Via Emilia. Asking Basinio about this, he confirmed it, saying furthermore that the Malatesta crest, being the elephant, derived from Scipio Africanus having, much later than those three battles, defeated such a mighty foe and taken in triumph from him the elephants which he had brought all the way from Africa to Italy for war. He told me also that Sigismondo openly admired the wiles of Ulysses, that Greek whom Dante placed in Hell for his deceptions, saying that it was he, not swift-footed Achilles or mighty Ajax, who had delivered Troy into the hands of the Greeks.
>
> At that moment a drum rolled, and all the assembly turned to look. Sigismondo advanced onto the open floor of the hall, in either hand a sword held vertically, surveying his audience to left and right as he came. Stopping before the centre of the floor he raised the blade in his right hand, saying "this was the sword of Alberico Novello da Barbiano, Count of Cunio, surrendered to me after the siege of Lugo." Turning to that in his left hand he said "and this fine sword belonged to that Pazzaglia slain at Esanatoglia in the Marches for having spoken against me." So saying he laid them before him on the floor, the one blade over the other in a cross. He turned back, and the drum took up again, joined by the *zampogna* in a rolling, martial tune. Sigismondo turned again, quickly, his head held high and haughty on his

neck's strong pillar to cast his glance over the assembly. Strutting forward, his hands held as fists on either hip, he leaped lightly to break into a fling over the crossed swords. Not once did he glance downward, not once did the sharp steel so much as nick the supple leather of his shoes. So did Sigismondo Pandolfo Malatesta display utter dominion of his enemies on the field of battle; so too did he commence the dances in celebration of the Castel Sismondo. As he danced I considered the two images, of Lancelot and of the Scipios, and saw in the pair an allegory of the balance of the soul of Sigismondo: in one scale he dreamed of being a Christian knight, as had I, while in the other he learned from pagan examples how to win, and in time that side outweighed his nobility and drove it from him.

It was in 1445, two years before that masque was held, that Sigismondo had been betrayed by Francesco Sforza. Galeazzo, son of Malatesta dei Sonnetti, sold Pesaro to Sforza who, being unsure of his succession to the Duchy of Milan, sought to expand his territory north from Ancona into the Romagna at that time. Leaving his brother Alessandro in charge of Pesaro, Francesco allied with Federico da Montefeltro - who had become ruler of Urbino the prior year, after the death of his father Guidantonio - and invaded the lands of Lord Sigismondo with a great force, far larger than might be mustered on our side. By 1446 he was besieging Gradara. Sigismondo knew well the strength of Gradara as a venerable stronghold of the Malatesta family. It was from here, Your Eminence, that Gianciotto Malatesta had ruled, who killed his wife and brother on discovery of their adultery and the poets put all three in Hell. Anyway, Sigismondo made a great show of gathering his troops, but without haste, as Sforza spent his gunpowder against the walls of Gradara. We set out, knowing ourselves outnumbered, on the march to relieve the beleaguered town.

Suddenly Sforza lifted the siege and retreated to Pesaro, and then moved out much of his force by ship. It seemed a miracle. Later it became known that Sigismondo had sent to Milan to convince Duke Filippo to recall Sforza, knowing that those strong walls of Gradara would not fall to Sforza's guns, and seeing no need to lead men to their deaths to achieve what could be won by words alone. Such guile is not applauded in all quarters, but from those of us whose lives were by such means spared it bought him loyalty.

Two years later Duke Filippo Maria Visconti of Milan died and there was the feud over the succession between Francesco Sforza and Alfonso, King of Naples and Aragon. Despite the attack by Sforza on our lands only the previous year, Lord Sigismondo initially approached the Florentines with an offer of service, but they refused him, going instead to Urbino and Montefeltro. Sigismondo then accepted a *condotta* from Naples, together with an initial sum of 27,000 ducats from which to raise and equip a significant force. These labours then occupied us through the winter.

The next year Giannozzo Manetti, a humanist of repute, came from Florence to Rimini as we were finalising our preparations of hiring, assigning and appointing, equipping where necessary. He requested an audience with Sigismondo, which was immediately granted. Manetti told Sigismondo that the Florentines had realised their error in not placing him in charge of the defence of the Tuscan territories. He said that they had always recognised his talents, but had feared them also, imagining that he might seize control of their Republic with ease through his famed martial prowess. Now, however, they saw that they had impugned his honour as an Italian to think so, and that the real threat to their liberty lay with the foreigner who ruled in Naples. Manetti told Sigismondo that he was empowered by the *signoria* to beg the famous captain to reconsider, to return the funds of his *condotta* to Alfonso and to come over to the Florentines for the defence of Piombino.

We who witnessed the scene fully expected that Sigismondo would reject Manetti's plea: the Aragonese were a great power next to whatever support the Florentines might purchase, and anyway the deal was already done, monies paid and spent. But Sigismondo stalled, saying that if he came over to the Tuscan cause then both he and his rival, Federico da Montefeltro of Urbino, would be on the same side. Had the Florentines not promised to Federico the position of captain of the forces defending Florence, and so Piombino?

At this Manetti paused, and then asked for three days in which to visit Urbino. He said that he would go to apologise to Federico that he must cede command now that Sigismondo Pandolfo Malatesta fought for Florence. Sigismondo smiled and acquiesced. Manetti bowed, took his leave, and set out for Urbino forthwith.

I confess that I was bemused. That Sigismondo would toy with an enemy was fully as I expected. Manetti, however, was a scholar, of the kind Sigismondo would ordinarily treat with respect; why should he dishonour Manetti so? Then it occurred to me that this course delayed the receipt in Florence of their answer by an additional three days, and furthermore kept busy their ambassador who was trying to raise aid for our opposition. I acknowledged that still such tactics were apparent to me only in hindsight.

We continued our preparations, mustering now for departure. On the third day Manetti returned, sought and was granted an audience, and informed Sigismondo that Federico da Montefeltro had agreed to serve under Sigismondo if he accepted the Florentine *condotta*. Sigismondo now had sown the first seeds of resentment between Federico and his employers, and Manetti could be sent off to Florence having achieved only a result in favour of us, his opponents.

To my astonishment Sigismondo instead approached Manetti, clasped his hands, and told him that he accepted the offer and would come over to the defence of Florence, leaving for Piombino to fight for her liberation. I was more shocked than Giannozzo Manetti appeared to be. I strove to see the hidden wisdom of this course, but it remained occluded.

No further explanation was offered by Sigismondo, even following Manetti's departure. We rode out over Tiberius' ancient bridge to form up our forces at the north side of Rimini, then made our way past Cesena to Forlì. There we stayed for the night before taking the turn off the Via Emilia where we would leave Malatesta lands through the hills for Tuscany. That evening, chancing on an opportunity to speak to Sigismondo alone, and noting how I endeavoured to learn from his talent for tactics, I asked if he would share with me his reasons why we were now to fight against Naples. Sigismondo looked at me, smiled just as he had to Manetti, and said "Ugo, are we not *condottieri*, fighting for pay in lands which are not our own, rather than patriots defending our native soil? Why then, let us be paid twice for the same service!"

From that time, Your Eminence, I ceased to think to learn military wisdom from Sigismondo Malatesta, but contented myself to serve, and so see how Fortune might treat with us.

We approached Piombino through Tuscany, joining with other forces in the pay of Florence as we went on. Montefeltro's force we did not meet until we were near to the Tyrrhenian coast, as he had come across keeping south of our lands. I did not see the two men together, and I think all their communications were by despatch.

We learned that the Aragonese had come with many galleys, intercepting all trading ships in the straits between the town and the island of Elba which lies opposite. By this means they prevented the town receiving support or supplies by sea. Had they not done this Piombino would be entirely unconcerned by the threat of siege from the landward side. Rinaldo Orsini, Lord of Piombino and Elba by marriage some three years before, and a very able soldier, had ensured that the defences of Piombino were sound, both strong and modern; but this was known to Alfonso, who had prepared a co-ordinated siege by both land and sea. We of course also knew that Alfonso's preparations assumed that we would form a significant fraction of their land forces; we therefore knew that we should now outnumber them on land. The outriders of our vanguard being seen by their sentries, they were forming up to face us as we approached the open ground of the fields inland of the walls of Piombino.

We simply formed up our lancers and rushed upon them. They had received no formal word that Sigismondo had changed sides, so that, even if rumour had reached them, the blow of its confirmation fell when they saw his standards carried towards them above the thunder of our charge. There was no discretion from Sigismondo here. This was the soldier we would respect in his caution and his wiles, because when the hour for valour and example came, he was not wanting. I spurred my horse but could not catch him as he rushed upon the forces of Naples. We outnumbered them in horse, as they were established for the siege, but what few they had came bravely on at us.

We closed, riding in a chevron. Sigismondo was off to my right, nearly but not quite foremost, with the one beyond him ahead by a horse-length. Some lancers of theirs, on fine Spanish stallions, directed their counter-charge here. I noted ahead of me that I was opposite their right flank, and that the men to my left would outflank them and continue unopposed to their infantry beyond.

I set my lance for the penultimate rider of their right wing, dark armour on a white horse, a shield bearing arms foreign to me. As we closed, I sensed suddenly that he was good, and the cold of fear rose up in me. His lance loomed towards my face as his stallion seemed to step aside in mid charge and I knew that I had lost him. I brought up my shield and braced, but the blow glanced upward with little force.

Lowering my shield again, I realised that just as his nimble mount had taken him away from me the man to my left, one Giovanni Falciano, had unhorsed him. The last man in their line had been dealt with by the riders beyond Falciano. Such are the advantages of numbers. We rode on, and routed their infantry; they fled around the southern end of the walls of Piombino, making for the shore and so the safety of their fleet. Some we rounded up, having overtaken them. Several of their lancers had been unhorsed but lived. All these we brought together in one place, on the road before the *Rivellino*, which is the strong main gate of Piombino, rebuilt by Orsini just the year before. Lord Sigismondo dismounted and approached them, encircled by our horsemen. They had thrown away their arms and simply stood, or sat, or lay, some looking apprehensive, some angered at their humiliation, some bored, awaiting the arrangements of their ransom.

Among their number was one who did not stand, but lay on the ground in full, fine armour. His helmet had been removed and he winced as he breathed. Sigismondo motioned to two of his own men who had followed with him to bring the man up. They got him to his knees before Sigismondo, who looked down into the man's face. He was not old, his hair and beard were black, his skin dark, whether Spaniard or from southern Italy I was not sure. Sigismondo started to talk. I am not a learned man, Your Eminence, and did not know the Latin. As he spoke, Sigismondo drew his sword, and at once, still talking to the man, plunged it down beside his neck, inside his armour and through all his vitals. All around both we and they stopped all movement, seized by fear and awe. Sigismondo withdrew his sword and walked away, and all of their number fell to the ground beseeching mercy.

One of the lancers on our side, but of the company of Urbino, called out to Lord Sigismondo, saying that this was a most unworthy act, to kill a surrendered foe, and not the manner in which a *condottiere* should behave. Sigismondo remounted his horse and told us that the man killed had been their foremost lancer in the charge, and had killed the man in our line to Lord Sigismondo's right, before being unhorsed by Sigismondo's lance. Montefeltro's man insisted that it was nonetheless unbecoming of a Christian soldier.

"Render unto Christ that which is Christ's, and unto Mars that which is Mars'. Pray to Christ for your immortal soul, but on the field of battle, War is God," said Sigismondo, and spurred his horse towards the *Rivellino* gate. As he passed before the man who had challenged him, he pulled up his horse, turned again to him and said "It may be that in centuries to come poor poets will sing us still, in cantos wrought to buy the favour of other little Dukes of Italy, thinking to make Virgils of themselves" and then turned and rode on. I was told later that the lines quoted by Sigismondo as he killed the unarmed man were from the poem of Aeneas

> by Virgil: "Pallas thus wounds you, Pallas takes sacrifice and retribution from your guilty blood."

Here two quotations are put into the mouth of Sigismondo Malatesta. The first paraphrases Christ's "Render unto Caesar that which is Caesar's and unto God that which is God's" from the gospels of Matthew (22:21), Mark (12:17) and Luke (20:25). For Sigismondo to traduce scripture, replacing the Christian God with Mars, speaks to his paganism. The quote from the *Aeneid* of Virgil is direct, from Book 12 verses 948-949. They are the words of Aeneas, known elsewhere as a paragon of piety, as he kills the defenceless Turnus.

> After that event my belief in my captain was shaken. I continued to fight for him, and again in the defence of Tuscany, when Alfonso's bastard Ferrante together with Federico da Montefeltro invaded again in the year 1452. But what had been cunning I saw now as base treachery, free of Christian restraint. Upon the consecration of the rebuilt church in Rimini I saw that he had made of it a pagan temple to deify himself and his mistress Isotta degli Atti. In 1454 I saw how his betrayal of King Alfonso six years before, defiant and proud, had led him to be excluded from the Peace of Lodi, such that Naples reserved for herself the right to war on Sigismondo. The following year I saw his refusal to engage the enemy at Siena which has so enraged the Holy Father. There was a time when I would have trusted that this was some ploy learned from Hannibal, perhaps as at Cannae, but no longer. I gave up soldiering after that campaign, retiring to my little farm at Balduccia. That was six years ago now, and I can tell you no more of Sigismondo Pandolfo Malatesta.

The reference to Cannae concerns another of Hannibal's famed victories over the Roman Republic. Here Hannibal withdrew his centre in good order immediately upon engaging the Roman infantry. When they then advanced, his flanks encircled, hemmed in and destroyed the superior forces of consuls L. Aemilius Paulus and G. Terentius Varro. Clearly this follows from the comparison previously made by Ugo of Sigismondo's tactics with Hannibal's victory at the Trebbia. The slaughter at Cannae was infamous as the greatest loss of life in a single day of battle in all of history until it was outdone, many times in succession, by the mechanised slaughter of this most recent disagreement between the civilised nations of Europe.

Thus ends Niccolò Perotti's transcription of the account of Ugo Tedeschini of Balduccia. It was provided entirely without further comment by Perotti. While many of the details accord with what is known of the military campaigns of Sigismondo Malatesta from other sources (the chronicle of the Malatesta by Gaspare Broglio, or '*Un Condottiere au XVième Siècle*' by Monsieur Yriarte are here examples of the first rank), and indeed of his character and personal passions, there are also many oddities and incongruities, some of which appear, to say the least, highly improbable. We must now consider the possibility that Ugo Tedeschini and his testimony were merely fruits of the imagination of Niccolò Perotti.

Perotti had been an underling to Bessarion. By the age of 18 he was serving as secretary to the Cardinal, who would at that time have tended to depend upon Perotti as an amanuensis for composition in Latin. When Bessarion was appointed to administer Bologna as Papal Legate in 1450, Perotti followed and from 1451 to 1453 taught rhetoric and poetry at the university. It was towards the end of this period that Perotti sent an assassin against Poggio Bracciolini, having taken the side of Lorenzo Valla in their dispute. When the attempt failed Bessarion forced Perotti into an apology to Poggio, who was by that time Chancellor of Florence. Perotti was, however, freeing himself from dependence on Bessarion's patronage: Frederick III, Holy Roman Emperor, had made Perotti his Poet Laureate in 1452 following Perotti's composition of a poetic welcome address for the Emperor; in 1455, upon the election of Alphonso da Borgia as Pope Callixtus III in preference to Bessarion, Perotti became Callixtus' secretary. It may therefore be the case that Perotti had personal reasons for misleading Bessarion. We should not necessarily regard him as a reliable source.

Moreover, Perotti may have intended Bessarion to recognise as much. The peculiarities noted, for example of Tedeschini's comparisons of Sigismondo with Christ, may have been obviously false to Bessarion, or the allusive significance transparent of references to Italy's glorious past as the homeland of the Roman republic through characters such as Cicero and the Scipios, or of the western martial prowess embodied by Lancelot. It is unfortunate that the inferences Perotti may have intended his reader to draw are largely lost to us, not least because without them the issue is less clear than it might have been. While this hypothesis cannot be proved, neither should it be dismissed.

Figure 6: "*Pallas te hoc volnere*", drawing by A.B. Cromar

The First Letter of Nicholas of Cusa,

Vicar-General of the Papal States, to Cardinal Bessarion, January 1462

This letter is the earlier in the collection of two by Nicholas Cusanus ('of Cusa', a Latinisation of his home town of Kues, which sits on the Moselle in the territory of Trier). Cusanus was a churchman two years older than Basilios Bessarion, having been born in 1401. He was also a scholar in the vanguard of humanism amongst the Germans, having been educated at Heidelberg, Padua, Cologne and Paris.

Cusanus' intellectual instincts lay in a universalising tendency which extended to a view of all religions as imperfect human attempts to apprehend the truth of God. He had great sympathy with the tradition of apophatic theology of the Orthodox Church, which asserts that God is unknowable, although in Cusanus' own conception, God, while infinite and therefore incomprehensible, is also "the one most simple essence of the entire universe" (quoted from his 'On Learned Ignorance').

The same impulse lay behind his argument that the Donation of Constantine was a forgery, ahead of Lorenzo Valla's more detailed philological argument of 1440 (being an example of Valla's application of philology to sacred texts which had led to his quarrel with Poggio Bracciolini). This was a concession of sorts to the Orthodox faction at the Council of Basel. Cusanus clearly ran the risk of crossing the line into heresy with this attitude. Indeed, he thanks Bessarion for his support in some such circumstances in his preamble to this letter:

> I recall with gratitude your assistance in the those matters of debate in which some of my writings had been misinterpreted as potentially heretical.

This followed from an attitude sufficiently inclusive initially to have extended to Islam, recognising it as an approach to the same God, albeit mistaken in detail. With the fall of Constantinople and reports of atrocities he changed his mind, as laid out in his 'On the Peace of Faith' of 1453. By the time of this letter he had moved radically away from conciliarism towards support of Papal authority, probably in part as a consequence of experiencing the intractability of the Council of Basel itself.

In 1449 he had become Cardinal-Priest of the Basilica of Saint Peter in Chains, then, in 1450, Bishop of Brixen in the Austrian Tyrol, and in 1459 Vicar-General of the Papal States. This last position meant that the intransigence of Sigismondo Malatesta as Vicar of Rimini fell within Cusanus' purview: it was in this capacity that Pius required his assistance as described in this letter rather than any particular theological or personal suitability to the task.

His letter is written in Ecclesiastical Latin. I have quoted in translation the larger part of it below, although some passages I have summarized or paraphrased in my interspersed commentary notes. After an introduction noteworthy only for the expression of gratitude towards Bessarion given above, he commences with the purpose of his letter thus:

> Sources abound, Your Eminence, attesting to the wickedness of Sigismondo Pandolfo Malatesta. These inform the list of crimes contained within the declaration of Andrea Benzi: the murders, betrayals and destructions inspired by greed; the adulteries, rapes and degradations driven by libidinous perversion; the desecrations and destructions of Holy sites; the eating of meat during Lent while in low company; the Epicureanism and the denial of both the existence of God and the immortality of the soul. Sigismondo Malatesta is accused of murdering his first two wives, Ginevra d'Este by poison, and Polissena Sforza by strangulation. And so on and so on.

Nicholas' letter proceeds with an immediate catalogue of the sins of which Sigismondo had been accused. The effect is adequately shocking that one might fail to notice that Cusanus here neither names any of the sources of these accusations, nor makes any claims to believing them himself. The Andrea Benzi mentioned here was the lawyer initially instructed by Pius to prepare the case against Sigismondo. Nicholas' '*Et cetera*' stands alone as a sentence set apart from the foregoing: I have translated it 'And so on and so on' to give a sense in English of what I read as a veiled indication of Nicholas' low opinion of the testimonies against Sigismondo.

Cusanus continues with a detailed account of the degradation of relations between Sigismondo and Pius. He starts with Sigismondo's 1459 agreement, brokered by the Pope, to pay Naples 50,000 ducats compensation for breaking the *condotta* of 1447. Note that the sum of 27,000 ducats paid by Naples at that time had 'acquired some interest' in the intervening years. Sigismondo was required to cede to the Pope several minor vicariates of his territories together with their strongholds as initial security against this sum, and also to return to Federico da Montefeltro a number of castles Sigismondo had captured.

Needless to say, Sigismondo did not remain bound by such constraints for long. In 1460 he and his brother Novello allowed Giacomo Piccinino to use Malatesta lands as a base from which to invade Neapolitan territory. Piccinino was backed by the House of Anjou, which sought to retake the Kingdom of Naples from the Aragonese. Sigismondo soon accepted Angevin support directly to besiege and capture those castles surrendered to the Holy Father only a year before, so rekindling his war against Federico da Montefeltro and Sforza in Pesaro.

Pius excommunicated the brothers Malatesta in December of 1460. He then proceeded to commission Benzi to compile the case against Sigismondo, with copies of the text of this accusation then being distributed to the various princes of Italy. When this failed to restrain Sigismondo, Pius requested Cusanus' assistance. Pius gave Sigismondo the opportunity to reply to his excommunication and the charges, to seek atonement and come to terms by which the two men might be reconciled. This was ignored. Sigismondo was subjected to a second excommunication in April of 1461. Sigismondo's reported response was to inquire whether food and wine lost their flavour for the excommunicated.

Cusanus reports that Pius sought from him

> a stronger tonic. His Holiness has, in the time in which he has occupied the Holy See, canonised only one saint into heaven, this being Catherine of Siena, only last summer. He asked me why, if the Vicar of Christ has the authority to send a human soul into Heaven, theoretically while still living, he should not also be empowered to send one to Hell, albeit, again, the soul of a living person?

> There were two aspects to my involvement, the first being the mundane business of extending the case against Sigismondo. Here there is no ambiguity: the fact is that those crimes initially listed by Andrea Benzi were sufficient to see Malatesta ten times damned. Nonetheless additional witnesses, such as the noble princes Federico da Montefeltro of Urbino and Alessandro Sforza of Pesaro, testified to further crimes of Sigismondo Malatesta which were then included in the revised accusations. From these testimonies the Holy Father went on to add his commentaries to Benzi's charges, with details of Sigismondo's rape of his own daughters and his son-in-law, of the killings of young boys who refused to play the bride for him, a role which Sigismondo himself had assumed, coupling with men and women indiscriminately, playing both roles with equal enjoyment. The Holy Father pointed out that this evil had spread throughout the whole Malatesta clan, from Malatesta Verrucchio down through the generations. He noted Paulo Malatesta's adultery with his brother Giovanni's wife, Francesca, and the deformed, jealous Giovanni's subsequent murder of the illicit couple. The poet Dante places all three in Hell: the Holy Father asserted that Sigismondo was merely the latest of his family destined for this fate. As to the reason, the sickness which ails a man that he should display so little regard for his soul, the Holy Father diagnoses the godlessness of Epicureanism.

There are several points of note here. Firstly, there is the obvious partiality of both Federico da Montefeltro of Urbino and Alessandro Sforza of Pesaro as witnesses against Sigismondo. Under our own legal systems such testimony would be 'laughed out of court'. I suggest the presence of irony in Cusanus' description of these as "noble princes", although we should remain aware that we are dealing with different times and different mores.

Secondly, I would observe that there is a clear propensity toward crimes of a sexual nature in those which Pius added to Benzi's original charge-sheet. The famous Viennese champion of psycho-analysis, Doctor Sigmund Freud, would surely have much to say on the matter. I am unqualified in the field, but I will note that this same predilection may be observed in the sermons of Aeneas Piccolomini's countryman, Bernardino of Siena, mentioned by Cusanus below.

The infidelity of Francesca and Paulo Malatesta is famously recorded by Dante in Canto V of the *Inferno*. Note that in Ugo Tedeschini's mention of this incident with respect to the castle of Gradara in the letter of Niccolò Perotti, Giovanni is named as Gianciotto, a sobriquet which he owed to his lameness.

Cusanus also mentions Pius' accusation of Epicureanism, discussed in my notes to the letter of Poggio Bracciolini as, in effect, the contemporary term for atheism.

From here Cusanus continues to a discussion of the nature of damnation:

> This touches upon the second, more interesting dimension, this being the theological aspect. You are aware that it had been my personal conviction that Hell need mean no more than perpetual exclusion from the light of God. You may also know that Holy Father Pius holds Hell to be a place of the active punishment of sins, as in the Florentine Comedy: he has had this conviction since the days when he was still Aeneas Piccolomini and heard the sermons of his compatriot Saint Bernardino. By this argument the issue becomes that the soul of Sigismondo Malatesta will reside in Hell while his body is observed to walk above the earth; the contention is that a demon animates the corporeal Sigismondo, having taken possession of him through his sinful nature. The remedy for the pollution of this world by one who in the proper order belongs in Hell must be to burn the body: if it is animated by an inhuman devil, this evil is thereby cast out of this world and returned to infernal darkness; if it is indeed still Sigismondo Malatesta who enervates that flesh, he shall rightfully be damned.

This Saint Bernardino is that Bernardino of Siena mentioned above, Bernardino degli Albizeschi. With a *floruit* in the early part of the *quattrocento*, Bernardino was a populist preacher of the type Savonarola would later emulate, although the sexual mores of women were a particular predilection of Bernardino. It is from this compatriot that Aeneas Piccolomini appears, somewhat before his election to the papacy, to have learned the misogyny and obsession with sexual crimes which characterise his discussion of Sigismondo Malatesta here and in his 'Commentaries', and which contrast so markedly with the writings of his frankly libertine youth.

In Canto XXXIII of the *Inferno* Dante describes meeting, in the ninth circle of Hell, the soul of a friar, one Brother Alberigo, who asks the poet how his body fares, it being still alive in the world above. This appears to be the model Pius had in mind for the damnation of Sigismondo Malatesta.

With no sign of contrition on the part of Sigismondo Malatesta, Cusanus goes on to describe the ritual proposed for this unique invert canonisation of the soul of a living person, to be performed in the coming spring:

> The Bull to be read will be a revision of the previous documents first prepared by Andrea Benzi a year past. By the authority of the Holy Father it shall be decreed that Sigismondo Pandolfo Malatesta be burned. For want of his person this shall be performed as ritual, in effigy, threefold throughout the following squares of Rome: the Capitoline, the Field of Flowers, and before the Basilica of Saint Peter. From the mouths of these effigies shall run inscriptions bearing the words "Sigismondo Malatesta, son of Pandolfo, king of traitors, hated of God and man, condemned to the flames by the vote of the Holy Senate." Further shall be set on his hat and beneath his feet the motto "Sigismondo Pandolfo Malatesta of Rimini, heretic." The same moment will see all pyres put to flame.

Cusanus proceeds to confess to Bessarion that there are those within the Vatican who have referred to this ceremony as a carnival. He expresses his own doubts regarding the reality of Hell, as opposed to it being merely the state of exclusion from the grace of God, and the difficulty he has in believing in the necessity of such torments in the service of unbounded love. He tells Bessarion that he nonetheless stands by the condemnation of Sigismondo Malatesta because he recognises his own human fallibility, and, moreover, has found something of interest in the arguments of Saint Bernardino:

> While men such as Your Eminence and my poor self have known the danger of vanity in our intellect, being aware of great scholars led into error by presumption, now

> Bernardino perceives a change in strategy from the Devil and his legion. While the Dark One may yet prey upon the learned, making wizards of them, now Satan preys upon those we had thought innocently unaware, but who Bernardino has noted have often a higher regard for their faculties than they merit: they are ignorant of their ignorance. Especially prey to these unholy wiles are, of course, women, through their tendency to superstition and the weakness of their minds and characters: thinking that they follow Diana, Proserpina or Hecate, rather Satan makes witches of them.

Here I must confess myself suspicious that Bernardino found in uneducated women a target less ably defended than the learned scholar who would typically be, in addition, a fellow churchman. This ungallant aspect of the argument is, however, peripheral:

> Whether we consider the learned or the ignorant, the noble or the base, the male or the female, the sin which allows the diabolical powers to corrupt a person is invariably the weakness of pride: so Bernardino of Siena preached, and here I cannot but agree. Sigismondo Malatesta is so full of this sin that I have found myself persuaded of the plausibility of the argument that he is surely possessed. This is the danger of the doctrine that "man as the measure of all things" as Plato tells us was asserted by the sophist Protagoras. It is, for me, the foundation of all Sigismondo's sin, the foundation of his conversion of a Christian church into a pagan temple in which he himself is deified. It allowed him to think himself the judge of his own soul, and so to free himself from all restraints of decency, and this arrogant pride has now cost him that very soul.
>
> The Holy Father must also act now because the fates of so many other Christian souls lie in the balance. Not only is there the desire to avoid conflict with Naples, and so Aragon, with the concomitant saving of many Christian lives and the avoidance of much suffering; there is also the need to preserve the polity of the States of the Holy See, which, to my mind, is this same issue writ large, indeed over all of Christendom. You are aware that I was in my youth in favour of the Council of the Church retaining the highest authority, providing that we distinguish between a *universal*

> council and a *patriarchal* council, as I recommended in 'The Catholic Concordance'. I reasoned that in this way more voices might be heard, from amongst learned authorities, and so the effects of human fallibility might be minimised. But I have now come to understand, as did Aeneas Piccolomini before he became Pius, that the infallible authority of the Holy Father is of supreme importance for the health of the Church Militant, which is the vehicle for salvation for all mankind, including the city of Constantinople and the lands of the eastern Christians.
>
> And so the damnation of Sigismondo Pandolfo Malatesta is imperative, and it is imperative that it be publicly declared. For if the excesses of such men go unpunished until after death, it will surely be that they will lead other men to their souls' doom. That Malatesta deserves Hell cannot reasonably be doubted, but, more than that, it is imperative that he repent or be damned immediately, for the danger he represents is the same one for which Dante put Ulysses so deep in Hell; that, like Satan, he leads other men to their doom with his falsehoods. It is needful in these times to see Christendom united under the Holy Father's direction for her defence. Her princes must be persuaded to direct their efforts and expend their energies in the service of Christ, given the encroachment into Europe of the Turk. Along the Danube, hard pressed by the Sultan's forces, Christian lands are defended by such as Vlad Dracul, Prince of Transylvanian Wallachia, but his heroism receives no assistance from the rest of Christendom due to her internal disunity. This in turn is a consequence of the example of Sigismondo Pandolfo Malatesta, who Posterity will surely confirm as the wickedest man of his age.

The omission which glares most brightly from this Cusanus' letter is the reason why he must explain himself to Bessarion. No doubt the men held each other in esteem, and, as noted here in his preamble, Nicholas had reason to be thankful to Bessarion. However, Cusanus is treading dangerously, expressing doubts with regard to the Pope's canonization into Hell of Sigismondo Malatesta which could be held against him at some later date. The obvious explanation for his confidence in Bessarion would be that his fellow cardinal was already implicated: might we imagine that the person who proposed the idea of this unique inverse canonisation to an irate Pope Pius had been none other than Basilios Bessarion himself?

Figure 7: Medal by Matteo de' Pasti of the winged eye sigil of Leon Battista Alberti, drawing by A.B. Cromar

The Letter of Leon Battista Alberti,

The Letter of Leon Battista Alberti to Cardinal Basilios Bessarion, May 1462

Leon Battista Alberti was perhaps the model for the modern term 'Renaissance Man', half a century before Leonardo da Vinci. He was powerfully athletic, skilled in the practice of literature, painting and architecture, writing on the theoretical underpinnings of these arts as well as grammar, cryptography, the family and other subjects.

Although of a wealthy Florentine family, he was born in Genoa (in 1404) due to his father having been exiled. Schooled in Padua and then studying law at Bologna, he took holy orders and entered the Papal Curia in 1431. He took great architectural interest in the classical ruins of Rome, before his first return to Florence in 1434.

As he mentions in this letter, the Florentine Renaissance had its first bloom of by that time, and Alberti engaged with it completely. Building on, among other things, Brunelleschi's demonstrations of geometric perspective, in 1435 he wrote *De pictura,* ('On Painting') his scholarly treatise on painting intended for patrons of the arts, with a version in the Florentine vernacular for artists, *Della Pittura,* following in 1441.

Following an architectural commission to design the facade of the Rucellai palace in Florence in 1446, he was then engaged by Sigismondo Malatesta for the redesign of the Church of St. Francis in Rimini, although the building work was actually overseen by Matteo de' Pasti. Alberti's treatise on architecture, *De re aedificatoria*, was completed in 1452, and was joined by *De statua* on sculpture a decade later: Alberti is more remembered for his books (these three being far from his complete bibliography) and their influence on other artists, than for his own architectural or artistic works. Had Sigismondo secured sufficient funds to complete the *Tempio Malatestiano* according to Alberti's design, that might have turned out differently.

His letter is written in a classicising Latin similar to that employed by Poggio Bracciolini. It commences:

> Spring, Your Eminence, I have ever thought the loveliest of the seasons. The snow has fled; the grass returns to the fields, the leaves to the trees; the earth changes and the streams pass their banks in fading spate. Zephyrus, messenger of Eros, seizes Chloris, transforming her to fecund Flora. The Graces awaken. I love the countryside, the wooded hills, the green valleys, and everything which grows there, flaming rose and timid mouse, lofty oak and lowly mushroom, not for their utility to man, but for their excellence within themselves. The incarnation and the crucifixion of our Lord changed everything of existence for mankind, but the rest of creation is just as it was for the ancients.

With this Introduction, which includes a verbatim quote of the opening of Horace's Ode 4.7 ('The snow has fled […] fading spate') Alberti initially appears merely to display his humanist erudition in support of his personal affection for the vernal. However, he continues with a quote from Lucretius' 'On Nature' (5.737-739: 'Zephyrus […] the Graces awaken') This is the passage which would later inspire Botticelli's *Primavera* and other works. Today we see little contentious in such portrayals of nature's fecundity, but Alberti is here quoting from that pagan text which was identified as the epitome of godlessness. He is careful to couch it in his personal appreciation of spring, quoting Horace first so that Lucretius' words appear only as further apposite poetic learning. He then affirms his fundamental Christianity ('The incarnation […] changed everything […] for mankind') to ensure that he is above theological reproach despite displaying his learning and aesthetic taste.

> In respect of theological truth, reason cannot avail us, only revelation; for all else which is not shown to us by scripture we must read the book of nature. Here reason is a surer guide, but still must follow and serve observation; are we not made in the image of God, and so, while we surely should not disparage the lessons to be found in old writings, shall we not learn also through careful attention to what comes to us through the senses, the wisdom of a more voluptuous Minerva?

With "*Minervae pinguioris*" (which I give as 'a more voluptuous Minerva') Alberti repeats his striking metaphor from *De pictura:* it is also found in the vernacular of *Della pittura* as "più grassa Minerva". His fondness for this incongruous image of a Rubenesque goddess of wisdom to embody his belief in the primacy of the sensual, the evidence of the senses, of observation, was an earthy and also lighthearted expression of the Franciscan tradition exemplified by such as Roger Bacon and William of Ockham. This is the birth of the modern, scientific attitude. Note, however, that Alberti is careful to make clear that this applies only outside of the area of theology which is addressed directly by Biblical revelation: we have no justification retrospectively to apply modern atheistic ideas to Alberti, Bacon or Ockham, all of whom were priests of the Roman church.

> I cannot tell you anything of Sigismondo Malatesta as a soldier, nor indeed can I tell you whether he will now be brought to heel by this carnival staged on the piazzas of Rome. In the matter of the damnation of Sigismondo Malatesta I will, however, make two observations. The first is that the Holy Father has not seen with his own eyes the crimes of which he accuses Sigismondo. The second is that the men who claim to have witnessed these transgressions are known enemies of Sigismondo, who stand to profit by his fall. When many of the black deeds listed were said to have been committed, no voice was raised against Malatesta in accusation at that time.

Here Alberti's purpose becomes clear: all of the foregoing has been in leading to this criticism of Pius' accusations against Sigismondo Malatesta. It is an appeal to Bessarion, as a man of independent mind, to recognise Sigismondo's trial as "a carnival".

> I do not mean to say by this that the Holy Father is wrong, for I myself have seen little of Sigismondo Malatesta. As I undertook in response to the questions which you put to me at our last meeting, I shall endeavour to tell you what I know of the man from my dealings with him in respect of his rebuilding of the Church of Saint Francis at Rimini, which many now call the Malatestan Temple in accusation of paganism.
>
> I have seen what Agostino di Duccio has made of the interior. Its allegories may be more sophisticated than our fathers saw in Italy, but they are no less Christian for that. Must our churches be forever filled only with crude

> instruction for the dullest minds? Those who accuse Agostino and Sigismondo are not drawn from the illiterate peasantry, and know well the zodiacal and astrological as a vocabulary for the wonder of divine creation.
>
> For all that, I recognise in the work of Agostino and Matteo the charge against Sigismondo of the sin of pride, everywhere the S entwining the I, and, in place of images of Christ and the Virgin, reliefs of Isotta and Sigismondo multiply. But is it not fitting that a Christian Prince, having rebuilt a church to the glory of God, might build also a chapel and a tomb within to encourage after his death the people to include in their prayers the fate of his immortal soul?

It was Agostino di Duccio who carved the limestone reliefs which adorn the interior of the *Tempio Malatestiano*. They are possessed of a fluid grace which is the Mediterranean petrified, their effect as much a consequence of their material as their design. Matteo de' Pasti was the builder of the *Tempio* to Alberti's design.

> It was in the year 1447 when I first went to Rimini to advise on the architecture of the rebuilding of that church. Malatesta was at the peak of his reputation as a *condottiere*, this being just prior to his betrayal of King Alfonso of Naples in the Tuscan war. Prior to that time his architectural spending had been, as that of his family ever was, on strongholds and fortifications, not least his *Castel Sismondo* at Rimini. He had but little use for men such as me in these enterprises, Your Eminence, for these buildings are determined by the cannon and the bombard, the ladder and the ram. In such a role I can imagine only that they excel, and indeed I had no reason to feel anything other than the intimidating strength of *Castel Sismondo* when I stayed there.
>
> The castle is built up against the landward walls of Rimini, facing into the town. It presents a severe aspect, although set at the same level as the town itself, the land being flat, unlike many other of the Malatesta strongholds. It is set back from the other buildings, separated by open ground and a moat.

While Alberti is correct that the fortresses built by the various branches of the Malatesta family throughout their territories and over the generations were determined primarily by military technology, Alberti is here disingenuous with regard to architectural influences on *Castel Sismondo*. It was Sigismondo's palace as well as his stronghold, *cf.* the testimony of Ugo Tedeschini. It may be that Alberti is here dismissive of rivals, although some sources assert that these included Brunelleschi himself.

> I must compare it to the palace at Urbino, for I have worked there for Sigismondo's rival, Federico da Montefeltro, in the time since. Montefeltro's palace is in the new style. It allows for defence, as does Castel Sismondo, but also for beauty and harmony of design, and indeed for the association of the Prince with his people, both aspects lacking in Sigismondo's fortress of the old style. The architecture of Federico suggests a prince who is a benevolent father to his people, while the Castel Sismondo appears the abode of a tyrant. I do not know that any such distinction between the rule of the two men exists in fact, but in these matters the impression engendered may be the most significant thing, hence the importance of the craft of the architect.
>
> It is to be allowed that Federico had the advantage of commencing his building later, once the ideas of the new style had become known. For, my family having been exiled from our home of Florence, I must tell you of my awe and delight when first I visited that city in the service of Holy Father Eugenius in the year 1434, only a few before you would have seen it yourself, Your Eminence. On the Cathedral of Santa Maria dei Fiori alone, Brunelleschi was closing the dome, Donatello was completing his work on the facade, and Ghiberti had cast the first of his pairs of doors for the baptistry, while across the city other commissions were transforming her appearance with a style unprecedented in artistry and technical skill. It is no slight to the young defender of Rimini that, only a year after the cathedral of Florence was complete, he would build his castle in the style mastered by his forebears, with modernity considered only of terms of military engineering. Even his temple was an early application outside of Florence of the ideas which I had refined upon seeing what was being

created within our city, so Sigismondo perhaps suffers when compared to Federico his rival simply because he acted first.

The redesign of the church was to derive from the classical, and also to represent Rimini in some manner, that it not be seen merely to ape Florentine practice, or some ruin in Rome. And so I used the details and proportions of the Triumphal Arch of Augustus which still forms the southern gate of Rimini toward the Via Flaminia. The height is of course a matter which had to be addressed, because I was working around the existing building of two centuries before, with its gothic proportions. As a remedy for this I set the arches up as on a podium, except for the main door. The additional height and tall proportion of this central arch of the facade I addressed with a smaller door inset, with its own pediment reaching the height of the pilasters of the arches.

Down the sides of the building this theme was continued, of arches set up on the podium. These were not blind, allowing the older building and its gothic windows to be seen through the new arches. This gives an impression similar to the double rows of columns surrounding the *cella* as seen in some examples of the ancients. Basinio Basini da Parma, for his flattery of Sigismondo in Latin poetry, has already been granted first place here.

We had in mind a dome. I have written of my preference for the circular temple, and, following Filippo Brunelleschi's dome of Santa Maria dei Fiore, we thought to place one of similar size on this church of Rimini, to match that of the Church of Saint Mary and the Martyrs in Rome. Had Sigismondo's financial success continued as it was at the time of the design, I have no doubt it would have been executed: Matteo de' Pasti indeed had medals cast for its foundation in 1450 which showed the dome atop the building.

The Church of Saint Mary and the Martyrs is more generally familiar as the Pantheon.

My second visit to Rimini was shortly after this time, when I could see what had been done with my designs. I was met with great courtesy, hosted at the *Castel Sismondo*. The atmosphere was changed from four years before. Sigismondo was at this time perhaps at the peak of his domestic happiness. His second wife Polissena, daughter of Francesco Sforza, had in the intervening time died of plague, and so Sigismondo's open courtship of Isotta degli Atti, which was already established on my prior visit, now at least did not bring public shame to a lawful wife. Moreover, Isotta could now be allowed openly to partner Sigismondo, and had grown from a mere girl into a woman also.

I do not know that I had harboured any particular expectations regarding the Lady Isotta, and when I met her I was not initially impressed with her, either in beauty or in manner. After a short time I was, however, struck by a rare intelligence and spirit in her. The woman who has captured the heart of the great dissolute Sigismondo Malatesta would indeed appear to be a singular example of her sex. Being a woman, her learning was not broad, but she brushed aside the usual polite flatteries which etiquette requires, and went on to ask perceptive questions of my thoughts on the arts, from architecture to painting to optics and cryptography.

I saw again how the work on the Temple had progressed. While Matteo de' Pasti was clearly talented, the artist who contributed towards the Temple with whom I felt the greatest affinity was Piero della Francesca. I recognise that it may be that I thought of him as a younger brother, both of us being descended from the nobility of Florence, both sharing our interest in the application of mathematics to the arts and man's apprehension of the world.

As in architecture, where Poggio Bracciolini has recovered Vitruvius for us, it is clear that we can now outreach the ancients. The Moslem Alhazen having improved upon the optics of antiquity, what might Christian men achieve if they only determine to strive? On the isle of Murano in the Venetian lagoon the glass makers are mastering the creation of larger and clearer mirrors than ever were known of old, applying secret admixtures of metals to the glass, and reflective surfaces of tin and quicksilver. I have discussed with Piero the principles set out in *Della Pittura* of the

> geometry of vision. Shall not the phenomena of appearance succumb to the reason granted us by God?
>
> As an aside, Your Eminence, you should know that your painting is complete. Piero has executed it according to the composition which I sketched for you. I hope it will meet with your satisfaction when you have the opportunity to see it, and of course that it makes its intended impression upon its recipient.

I return to the issues of the identity and underlying purpose of this painting by Piero Della Francesca in my notes accompanying the second letter of Nicholas Cusanus.

> Piero has developed as an artist since he executed the fresco for the reliquary of the Malatestan Temple a decade ago. His skill to represent was very fine even then. You will see, though, how his *istoria* and his mastery of pyramidal perspective have developed.

I have left the word '*istoria*' untranslated, following its use in *Della pittura.* Alberti means by it something like "composition", including the placement and arrangement of persons within the space of the picture for the purposes of storytelling as well as aesthetic considerations. The 'pyramid' of Albert's perspective has its base set vertically as the scene represented on the plane of the painted canvas, and is apex at the eye of the beholder. This is then mirrored by the lines of perspective appearing to recede within the image towards the 'vanishing point'.

> The Malatestan fresco is a fine work, for its purpose, but, as with Sigismondo's castle, not new in its design. It shows a knight, kneeling in devotion before a saint. A shield bearing his arms is set above. Behind him through a window his fortress is seen. Below this his fine hunting dogs lie, the white facing right, the black left. So this fresco follows the traditions of the Christian knight. And yet the Saint is given the likeness of the Emperor. This is not a painting of the piety of one who rules as a vicar of the Holy See; this is a display of the magnificence of a knight of the Emperor. And then this knight is shown centrally, the Saint is set off to the extreme of the frame. It is not that the painting shows

> loyalties which are Ghibelline rather than Guelph, but that it shows a man who has no master but himself.

Alberti here reverses the directions of the hunting dogs as they appear to the viewer. He may simply be mistaken, describing from memory, or it is perhaps that he is using the terms as in heraldic convention, in which they are described relative to a figure facing towards the viewer.

> You will be aware that my work *De pictura* has two versions, written for two different audiences. The first, in Latin, was for those who view the works of art, that is the patrons. Then I wrote a vernacular edition, which was somewhat different, lighter on philosophy and classical allusion, heavier on practical techniques, being intended for artists themselves. This, I hold, is reflected in a comparison of Federico da Montefeltro and Sigismondo Malatesta.
>
> Federico is a great patron of the arts, Your Eminence, far outstripping Sigismondo. He has taste and judgement in the new style. Posterity will judge him the wiser, more humane man. But he will not himself inspire art. He will only consume it.
>
> Sigismondo Malatesta is something else. His castle is functional and artless. The poets of his court, Basinio da Parma, Roberto Valturio, and the rest, are sycophants and flatterers, mere imitators of the styles of others. His temple lies unfinished, having been conceived on a scale which, it transpired, was beyond his purse. The interior has been worked to his vision, without the restraint of good taste. His fresco is in a fashion which seems old already to us.

I find it difficult to determine whether Alberti genuinely held such a low opinion of the artistic taste of Sigismondo and his court, especially his harsh judgement of Basinio da Parma and Agostino di Duccio here, or it merely suited his present rhetorical purpose to argue this. Given the incongruity noted above in respect of the hunting dogs of Piero Della Francesca's fresco, and the oversimplification of his assessment of the architecture of the Castel Sismondo, I am swayed towards the latter view.

> If you think to make Sigismondo the tool of your craft, to write the book of your ambition with him as the quill, his

> blood for ink, I wonder, Your Eminence, if you are mistaken, and that he will ever slip beyond your grasp, as though some other hand already moves the pen to the design of some other mind? I put it to you that Sigismondo Malatesta is an artist, and his own life is his canvas, his own self his brush, and, wherever he may end, it will be he, not you or any other, who has moved him. I suspect him incapable of fear of the damnation to which he stands condemned, his mind being his own place to make of Pius' Hell his own Heaven.

The proposition that Bessarion's purpose with these letters was to provide the Cardinal with the necessary information to allow him to manipulate Sigismondo Malatesta for his own ends is here supported very strongly indeed. It remains to be established what those ends may have been, and there are now in addition the mysteries of the identification of the painting by Piero della Francesca, and the determination of the purpose for which Cardinal Bessarion appears to have commissioned it.

Figure 8: The Tempio Malatestiano as conceived by Leon Battista Alberti, frontal aspect, from a drawing by A.B. Cromar

The Letter of Vettore Cappello,

Savio Grande of the Republic of Venice, To Cardinal Basilios Bessarion, January 1464

Vettore Cappello was a Venetian military commander. Born in 1400, he was three years older than Bessarion: it is clear from the tone of this letter - as well as the choice of the Venetan language - that Cappello felt no obligation to make any great display of deference to the Cardinal. As the *lingua franca* of the areas of the Mediterranean under the control of the Venetian Republic, Bessarion would have had some familiarity with Venetan from his time in the Morea, as well as through his ongoing connections with Venice as the main conduit by which Byzantine refugees were entering Italy. Clearly Vettore Cappello felt sufficiently confident of Bessarion's comprehension to choose to write in his own native tongue.

From his family's trading business Cappello had moved into Venetian politics. By 1447 he was elected to the Council of Ten. This powerful body was covert even by the clandestine standards of the Venetian state, its annually selected members taking an oath of secrecy; it had power over military expenditure and, in 1355, had even ordered the execution of Doge Marino Faliero.

In 1454 Cappello had been ambassador to the Morea, intervening to reconcile Thomas and Demetrius Palaiologos with their Albanian subjects who had appealing to Venice to annex their lands. Venice, rather than encourage Ottoman intervention against Venetian territories, had declined.

On Cappello's appointment in 1461 as Captain General of the Sea (commander of Venetian naval forces), he succeeded in avoiding hostilities with the Turks while reinforcing the various Venetian fortified strongholds around the Peloponnese and the Aegean. By the date of this letter he had been appointed one of the six *Savii del Consiglio* - 'Wise Men of the Council' - with even more seniority within the Venetian state than the Council of Ten. He had also moved from the moderate to the pro-war faction.

His letter is brief, and I give its full translation here, albeit interrupted by my comments:

> Arts proper to a Prince must naturally include warfare. In this respect Sigismondo of Rimini is a gentleman of unparalleled refinement, and so, after due consideration, we endorse your proposal to employ him as captain of our land forces for the prosecution of the Morea campaign. His military abilities are well proven, and we concur that his family connections to the area should serve to motivate him to the action which, at times in past campaigns, he has shirked.
>
> You have satisfied us that Matteo de' Pasti, while certainly despatched from Rimini, was either making an ill-judged attempt at a commercial arrangement with the Sultan, or, if he was engaged in espionage, then at least it was not treacherous espionage against us. If indeed the vial in his possession contained holy water, then the harbour of Candia is now baptised.

In 1461 Matteo de 'Pasti, builder of the *Tempio Malatestiano*, had been intercepted in Candia - modern Chania, capital of Crete - by the Venetians as he tried to make his way to Sultan Mehmed. He had sailed from Rimini, thus apparently having been sent by Sigismondo Malatesta. The reference to a vial of holy water - which it would appear the Venetians simply threw into the harbour of Candia - is reminiscent of a proposal of Pius that the Pope would recognise the Ottoman Sultan as Eastern Emperor if he would only accept anointment by the smallest amount of holy water. While this suggests that the Pope may have been behind the scheme, it would apparently require co-operation between Malatesta and the pontiff as early as 1461, that is to say during the period of greatest public acrimony between the two men.

> With regards to the animosity felt by the Holy Father towards Malatesta, we shall be guided by your assurances that this course will serve to reconcile them, rather than lead to a division of purpose between our forces.
>
> The Holy Father himself, we understand, travels to Ancona to oversee the mustering of the troops of his own states under Skanderbeg. Our esteem for that captain of the Albanians is such that we have sent Antonio da Cosenza with five hundred horse and five hundred foot to serve with him. In the Bosnian territories, as you may already have

> heard, the Hungarians took Jajce on the sixteenth day of December. We are given to understand that Corvinus is now well established in that land, holding several dozen fortified places.

Skanderbeg, from the Turkish *Iskender Bey*, was Gjerj Kastrioti, anglicised as George Castriot, a member of the Albanian nobility. He served the Ottomans as a young man, but deserted them after the great Hungarian general John Hunyadi defeated the Sultan's forces at the Battle of Niš in 1443. Skanderbeg then united the Albanian people in national resistance to the Turks.

Following the Diet of Buda in 1462, King Stephen Tomašević of Bosnia accepted vassalage to Matthias Corvinus, son of John Hunyadi and King of Hungary and Croatia. He consequently stopped paying tribute to the Sultan. The Turks promptly invaded Bosnia, southern Hungary and Transylvania. Corvinus approached both Venice and the Pope, and these provided both financial and materiel support, as well as agreeing a mutual offensive and protective alliance against the Turks. Corvinus then drove the Turks back from Bosnia, including successfully recapturing the walled city and high fortress of Jajce after three months of siege in late 1463. It lies in what is today the Bosnia Vilayet of the Balkan territories annexed from the Ottomans by Austria-Hungary in 1878, some hundred miles proximal of Sarajevo, which was founded by the Turks around the time Vettore Cappello wrote this letter, and was of course where Gavrilo Princip's fateful act of idealistic murder a few years ago fulfilled Chancellor Bismarck's prophecy of "some damned foolish thing in the Balkans". Though four and a half centuries have elapsed, the war into which Cappello here accedes to conscript Sigismondo Malatesta has only now been peacefully settled through the creation of the state of Yugoslavia.

> In the Morea matters have gone less well. The gains of last year have been reversed. Ömer Bey has been strengthened by forces under the Grand Vizier. The Hexamilion is breached; Argos has fallen, and, we now hear, been razed. Alvise Loredan has requested repatriation. He is a man of seventy years now, and has served the Republic faithfully and well. We expect to replace him as Captain General of the Sea with Orsotto Giustinian. On land we shall have Malatesta.

The Venetian land forces, led by Bertoldo d'Este, had initially made significant gains in the Morea in early and mid 1463. Retaking Argos, they pushed back the Turks to the Isthmus of Corinth. Here they restored the Hexamillion ('Six Mile') Wall which spanned the isthmus, additionally installing guns along its length. The Turks, however, still held the high fortress of Acrocorinth to the Venetian rear. In besieging Acrocorinth, d'Este was killed. At this, and beset by dysentery, the Venetians became demoralised, retreating first to the Hexamillion and then to Nauplio. This was the situation which Sigismondo Malatesta was to inherit.

> The Doge is not encouraged, for we are Christian men, and Jove will not beget for us the Perseus for whom we cry. Rather the Holy Father must be drenched beneath the flow of sequins from the Grand Canal, that Malatesta might fly to Taygetos and break the Mystrian chains. *Amor vincit omnia et nos cedamus amore.*

Cristoforo Moro, Doge of Venice at this time, remained sceptical of the wisdom for Venetian interests of war with the Sultan. As noted above this had been Cappello's own position until shortly before the date of this letter.

Cappello closes with an extended metaphor by which he criticises Pope Pius II. Perseus was fathered on Danaë by Jove in the form of a shower of gold. Cappello laments that such heroes of classical myth are unavailable to them as Christians, and so Malatesta must substitute for Perseus and fly to the rescue of Mystras. Built up the side of the Taygetos, Mystras here corresponds to Andromeda chained to a rock face as the sacrificial victim of the monster Cetus, which, therefore, represents the Turks. Venice is required to provide the flow of gold in place of Jove, with the implication being that Pius takes the place of Danaë in Cappello's metaphor.

I translate as 'sequins' Cappello's word *zecchini,* the ducats issued by the *Zecca*, the state mint of the Republic which stood on the banks of the Grand Canal of Venice. The English word derives from the decorative practise of sewing *zecchini* onto the clothing and headdresses of ladies of social standing. It is not clear whether for Cappello this association would have furthered his feminising aspersions cast upon Pius.

Cappello's final Latin quotation is taken from the *Eclogues* of Virgil (10.69) and translates as 'love conquers all, let us yield to love'. Ostensibly Cappello refers to the love between Perseus and Andromeda. However, Cappello's purpose is to continue his criticism of the Pope. In 1444, before becoming Pope Pius II, Aeneas Piccolomini had written 'The Tale of Two Lovers', an epistolary erotic novel. The protagonist of that work, one Euryalus, quotes Virgil with this phrase in self-justification, before penning his first letter to his married lover Lucretia. As seen in the earlier of Nicholas Cusanus' letters, Aeneas had fiercely repudiated his youthful enthusiasm for such erotica by the time he was elected to the papacy, becoming puritanical and even misogynistic. In quoting this line here, Vettore Cappello extends his criticism of Pius through the use of erotic allusion.

This letter provides final, explicit revelation of Bessarion's plotting and his manipulation of Sigismondo. It may be that it was Bessarion rather than the Pope who was behind Sigismondo's dispatch of Matteo de' Pasti towards Constantinople; this would be more plausible given the acrimony between Pius and Sigismondo at that time. In any event we are shown here that it was Bessarion who proposed to the Venetians to give control of their land forces in the Morea to Sigismondo. Of course, this does not prove that this was actually Bessarion's idea: it is entirely plausible that Bessarion approached *La Serenissima* on the orders of the Pope. Having Sigismondo be part of the solution rather than part of the problem would have suited Pius, and keeping Sigismondo separate from Pius and his own forces under Skanderbeg would also be a requirement.

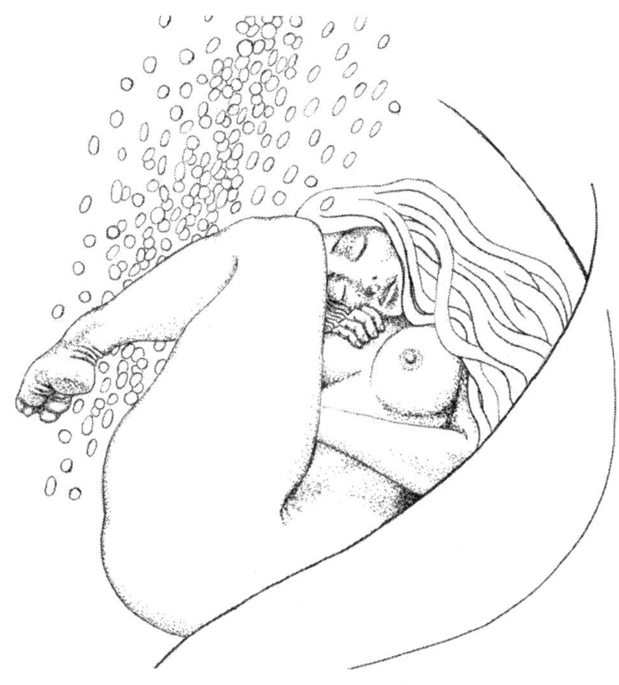

Figure 9: Danaë, drawing by A.B. Cromar after Gustav Klimt

The Second Letter of Nicholas of Cusa,

Bishop of Bressanone and Vicar General of the Papal States, to Cardinal Basilios Bessarion, July 1464

An outline biography of Nicholas of Cusa is given in my commentary on his earlier letter: this is the sole instance within the collection of more than one letter having been written by the same author. Writing in his usual Latin, Nicholas' opening address on this occasion is surprisingly informal:

> All my hopes are proved fruitful, old friend, by news that you are well. For my part I think the time may be upon me to put aside worldly concerns, preparing to pass beyond that veil which occludes our mortal comprehension. What I behold now as in a mirror, in an icon, in a riddle, shall it be granted to me to apprehend with the perspective of the infinite centre, the boundless boundary? Do not grieve for me as I pass away from the pettiness of the lords of this world. I shall set down some of my thoughts, which may or may not avail you, for you who must remain in this cave of shadows.
>
> The object of your concern, Sigismondo Malatesta of Rimini, campaigns now against the Turk in the Morea. He works the will of the Holy Father, acting for the Christian good. If he can be brought to true repentance he must, of course, have mercy: if by his service, turning his bellicose talents to the service of Christ, he may make his peace with the Holy Father, then naturally I would argue that his sentence be revoked. But, though he stands daily in the path of Mars, he stirs not one pace towards the salvation of his soul. I confess that I do not understand how a man can set so little store by the matter of eternity. Either he has no belief in heaven, being an Epicurean or Sadducee, or he spurns it as a devil. I do not know which I deem more terrible: to be blind to the light of God, or to turn away from it in hatred.

The Nicholas of Cusa of this letter is rather different from that of his letter of two years previously. There he is describing and justifying the process of the inverted canonisation of Sigismondo Malatesta, something he has been required to do, rather than something he has chosen. Here, in contrast, we have Cusanus writing on his own terms, apparently aware that his life's end is near, being his more usual contemplative and otherworldly self. He was to die the following month, while travelling from Ancona to Genoa on the orders of the Pope.

Cusanus' innate preoccupation with the spiritual prevents his comprehension of Sigismondo's behaviour, and of course Nicholas has been party to Sigismondo's damnation which, if not reversed before his death, will be irrevocable. The accusation of Epicureanism towards Sigismondo I discuss in my notes to Cusanus' earlier letter; the Sadducee disbelief in the soul's survival after bodily death is attested in, for example, The Book of Acts (23: 6-9) or Josephus' 'Jewish Antiquities' (18:1.4).

> Blindness surrounds us. You have been in communication with the celebrated Florentine Leon Battista Alberti. I know you to be wise, but here I must presume to beg you to have a care, dear Bessarion. For in the illustrious Messer Alberti, who instructs every man in how the world is to be seen, I myself see a terrible cyclopic myopia. He extends the contentions of the Franciscans to the detriment, I fear, of humility before God. The perspective for which he argues, which he teaches to the young painters, places a single human eye at the centre of all things: I refer you to his device. Thus he presents the world as the vision of man rather than of God, static and thereby eternal, assuming for man the infinite nature which is God's alone, denying to human apprehension anything of the enfolding of the Creator in his creation. This mirror of nature is dead, contrary to our experience of the world which is a living mirror of the divine, as is depicted in a true icon. I have written in 'On the Vision of God' of the congregation of the monks of Tegernsee, with a shared contemplation allowing us some sense, albeit limited, of the divine perspective. The all-seeing gaze exemplifies an impossibility that coincides with necessity. This is the knowing unknowing of finite human reason apprehending the infinitude of God, who exceeds all relativistic determinations and oppositions by necessity. The plurality of human perspectives is what

> demonstrates, as what is invisible to one is visible to another, the infinite nature of God's perspective. Through inflated scientific pretensions Alberti denies this, and leaves man alone in a lifeless world.

The influence of Franciscan nominalism on the thought of Leon Battista Alberti is not in doubt; indeed, he confesses as much in his own letter of this collection. Albert's 'device' of a winged eye can be seen, for example, on the obverse of the medal of 1450 by Matteo de' Pasti (from when the two collaborated on the construction of the *Tempio Malatestiano*). It epitomises his geometric conception which, in addition to the discipline of visual representation through his rules of perspective, can also be argued to have influenced the Cartesian and thence the Newtonian conceptions of the mechanics of the physical world. It is only in our present day that we meet significant challenge to such orthodoxies in, on the one hand, the attempted representation of multiple viewpoints of the 'cubist' painting style, and, on the other, the unsettling implications the ideas of Professor Einstein which suggest that the operation of physical laws themselves may not be absolute, but, rather, relative to the observer.

> I have heard of a device contrived by Alberti which is telling in this regard. Taking the cipher attributed to Julius Caesar, he mechanises it by means of two concentric disks, on each an alphabet inscribed. By rotation of the disks relative to each other, and the consequent juxtaposition of these two alphabets, any Caesarean cipher may be read thereon; so much the elements can bring about by change of order alone. Messer Battista Alberti claims that with this toy he has a cunning invention, but it is merely derivative of a machine of Ramon Llull derived from the *Xairja* of the Moors two centuries ago. The learned Doctor of Majorca, in his work to convert the Moslems to the true faith, made a device of *three* concentric wheels in which was encoded his Great Art. You will anticipate that I take issue with the good Doctor in that no engine of finite permutations, though they number greater than the grains of sand to fill the Empyrean, touches upon the infinity of God.

"I have heard of a device contrived by Alberti which is telling in this regard": this is a description of the 'Alberti Cipher Disk', described by Alberti himself in his 'On the Composition of Ciphers' of 1467 -

so three years after this letter. It consisted of two disks set concentrically on a common pin and so able to rotate relative to each other. The larger *stabilis* was divided into sectors containing the letters of the Italian alphabet corresponding to the text to be encoded, plus the numbers 1 to 4 to allow super-encipherment according to algorithms which Alberti set out in his treatise; the smaller *mobilis* had a corresponding number of cells for the letters of the cipher text. Alberti's encipherment methods were very substantially more sophisticated than the basic Caesar cipher Cusanus presumes the intention of the device to be: Nicholas is of course writing three years before Alberti published his methods, so this misunderstanding is forgivable.

Intriguingly, the words "so much the elements can bring about by change of order alone" are a quotation from *De Rerum Natura.* The 'elements', as Lucretius uses the Latin '*elementa*', refer both to the Epicurean atoms, but also to the rearrangement of letters to spell words differing "both in sense and ring of sound". Is this a further instance of Cusanus demonstrating to Bessarion his familiarity with classical, pagan literature, and in this case the poetry of the heretical Epicurean Lucretius?

Alberti credited his inspiration for his cipher disk to a conversation with the pontifical secretary Leonardo Dato about the new technology of the moveable type printing press, rather than Cusanus' contention that it derived from the *Ars Magna* of Ramon Llull. Llull was a Majorcan Franciscan of the turn of the thirteenth to fourteenth centuries whom Nicholas had studied at the University of Paris in his youth. Llull had expended significant effort towards the conversion of the Moors: like Nicholas of Cusa he believed in the essential similarity of all religions and all descriptions of God. This same impulse led Llull to his 'Great Art' by which he aspired to access the deepest truths. Its first incarnation was as a series of complex tables, but, when students found this impenetrable, a revised version took the form of a set of three concentric discs circumferentially divided, in the same basic form as Alberti's Cipher Disk. As Cusanus mentions, Llull's inspiration for this contrivance was the Moorish *Ziarja*, which took a similar form, and served a related function, but was essentially astrological in nature. The purpose of Llull's 'Great Art' tool was, through the juxtaposition of symbols by relative rotation of the discs, to answer any question posed: Llull's contention was that there could be only a finite number of these due to the fundamental simplicity underlying the apparent complexity of creation.

Nicholas of Cusa agreed with the notion of a fundamental underlying simplicity, but he held that this simplicity was that of God. However, this did not trivialise God, whose nature remained beyond human comprehension: Cusa characterised this as the distinction between the apparent complexity of the numerous aspects of the world and the simplicity of the infinite divine. This notion is what he is alluding to when he writes "the infinite centre, the boundless boundary". Thus, as he says, he remains unpersuaded of any insight available through Llull's device, although he sympathises with the aspiration, while disparaging Alberti's.

All three devices - that of the Moors, of Ramon Llull, and of Leon Battista Alberti - share the same intent of unveiling occult truth through the combinatorics of their concentric dials, reflecting a common interest in the magical science by which mere symbols combine into meaningful words capable of transmitting ideas: literally 'spelling'. The distinction is that in the first two cases the source of such truth is held to be God, while for Alberti its origin lies with man.

Cusanus' expression "though they number greater than the grains of sand to fill the Empyrean" appears to be a reference to the 'Sand Reckoner' of Archimedes of Syracuse which estimated just this quantity. The Empyrean is the outermost of the heavenly spheres, which in the Christian cosmology - as traversed by Dante in the *Commedia* - was the abode of God. Archimedes performed the calculation to demonstrate that the number, while large, was calculable and fundamentally distinct from infinity.

Many of the works of Archimedes were familiar to men of letters at this time, from a Latin copy Pope Nicholas V had commissioned of the manuscript of Johannes Regiomontanus. It was this same Regiomontanus who completed George von Peuerbach's commentary on Ptolemy's *Almagest* for Bessarion. It is probable that it was Bessarion who also had the 'Sand Reckoner' copied for the Pope. Is Cusanus indicating that he is aware of Bessarion's contributions to scholarship, whether out of flattery or subtly to demonstrate his own parity in this arena?

> Both of these issues, I maintain, demonstrate the underlying conceit, which is that all of creation is discoverable and comprehensible through human reason. This is a disastrous belief, full of hubris, which will lead men to Epicureanism and unbelief, as I have argued in 'On Learned Ignorance'. The threat is not only to the souls of those who follow this doctrine, for my contention is not that they will fail to gain mastery over nature and the created world, but rather that they will, like Sigismondo Malatesta, lose all moral restraint. Having no rule to their conduct, they will fill all God's creation with men become demons of great power and great evil, who will gain the power to destroy all mankind, but at the cost of all reason to love one other and so to restrain their lusts. For without God's truth, what shall not be permitted?
>
> No doubt you will laugh, dear Bessarion, at this uncultured German lacking the venerable learning of Italy and of Greece. But I can make my argument from the examples of your ancients themselves, who knew this type of man in Ulysses, the poet Homer's man of many ways. This is he who contrived the horse to which Troy fell, who presumed to travel even to Hell while living, who revelled in deceit and reviled the honour of his comrades. The Romans, to their credit, held him in low esteem, and Dante the Florentine put him in the eighth circle of Hell for eternity, for sailing into the western sea, thinking to go beyond the sunset, and so leading his crew to their doom. But in recent years the Portuguese Prince Henry directed crews to undertake just such voyages, endeavouring by sailing westward to find the Indies rather than their death. Even were they to succeed, or find some lands as yet unknown to Christendom out there beyond the sunset, what tales would we then hear truly told? What limits would such men place upon their ambition? Become masters of all land and sea, what might not they then attempt? To fly up in the sky as though to mock the angels? To set their foot upon the moon?

The Latin from which I have translated as 'what tales would we then hear truly told?' has "*historias*" for tales and "*vere*" for truly. In the context of voyages into the Atlantic I posit this as alluding to the

Ἀληθῆ διηγήματα, or 'True Story' of Lucian, commonly translated as the '*Vere historias*' in Latin. That great satirist's title, he tells us in his introduction, is in recognition that every word of his story is a fabrication apart from this admission, making him that rarest of creatures: an honest storyteller. He recounts a journey out into the Atlantic where new lands are found, amongst other outlandish locations, before being carried up into the air to the moon: cf. "to fly up to the heavens [...] set their foot upon the moon".

I additionally assert that this literary allusion fits with Cusanus' explicit purpose in this paragraph, which is to support his claims by appeal to his familiarity with literary examples. He has cited Ulysses as his example of the over-reaching man unfettered by humility. He has demonstrated his knowledge of Dante presenting Ulysses as damned for leading other men to sail out into the Atlantic to their doom through this fault. He follows this with the observation that "the Portuguese Prince Henry" has been sending contemporary crews to do the same, "by sailing westward to find the Indies". This is Henry the Navigator, fourth son of King John I of Portugal, who had died four years before this letter was written. He had been responsible for sponsoring Portuguese voyages of exploration down the west coast of Africa and out into the Atlantic.

To drop in a final, subtle allusion to Lucian - a writer in the Greek tradition of the eastern empire, amongst those recently rediscovered in the west due to the influx of Greek influence - would serve to impress Bessarion with Cusanus' knowledge of Greek literature. It would, through the ludic nature of Lucian's satire, provide a scathing, comic condemnation of the worldly vanity of the aspirations of men such as Ulysses, Prince Henry and so, too, Leon Battista Alberti. Of course, we know that the explorations supported by Henry the Navigator led directly to Vasco de Gama reaching India by sea in 1498, and informed the voyage of Columbus to the Americas in 1492.

However, Cusanus' point is not that these things are beyond human capability. Indeed Paulo dal Pozzo Toscanelli, who had known Nicholas since he studied law in Padua four decades previously, and who would be one of the executors of Cusanus' will a month after this letter, was also the man who, in 1474, created the chart of the Atlantic showing Cathay at its western shore which would inspire Christopher Columbus. Rather Nicholas questions what it is all for, and where such an all-conquering attitude to nature and the world may ultimately lead.

> Nobody who is unknowing can ascend to wisdom by his own light. For this reason, those who are proud-hearted, those who trust in their own intelligence, all these err, since they foreclose to themselves the path of wisdom when they deem there to be no other way than that which they measure by their own intellect. In their vanities they fall short, and embrace the tree of knowledge but do not apprehend the tree of life.
>
> I have heard of a little painting newly displayed in the palace of Urbino, painted by Piero della Francesca, disciple of Messer Alberti. It shows the flagellation of Christ, but relegates the suffering of our Lord to a detail of the background, all the remainder of the scene given over to the works of man, and rendered according to this human perspective taught by Alberti. Half of the image contains figures much larger than Christ himself, that attention might be drawn to this trick of composition and appearances. I should make you aware, Your Eminence, that my witness had thought that one of these figures bore a resemblance to you, although perhaps some years younger than you are now. I hope you are not to find yourself drawn into error by the tastes of Prince Federico.

The "little painting [...] painted by Piero della Francesca" Nicholas refers to is, I propose, the same painting mentioned by Leon Battista Alberti in his letter. Moreover, I contend that with the details provided here it can be identified as Piero della Francesca's 'Flagellation of Christ' which hangs in Urbino to this day. It has been described by some art historians of standing as the greatest small painting in the world. As Cusanus describes, Christ is relegated to the background of the left of the painting, in a contemporary interior space depicted with severe geometric perspective. The right of the image is dominated by three foreground male figures in *quattrocento* dress. Their identities are not agreed, but the leftmost of the three has been proposed as an image of Basilios Bessarion.

On the evidence of Alberti's letter, it was painted by 1462. This makes the 'Flagellation' earlier than the same artist's 'Legend of the True Cross' fresco series for the Basilica of San Francesco in Arezzo which was finished in 1464. While it is still considerably later than his fresco of *Sigismondo Malatesta and Saint Sigismund* in the *Tempio Malatestiano* (painted in 1451), it is early for such a marked example of Alberti's rules of geometric perspective being used to give the appearance of depth within a scene. That Leon Battista Alberti may have played some part in its composition would be of a piece with this.

Nicholas of Cusa's objections to Leon Battista Alberti's mathematical rules of visual perspective may appear overwrought to us today, and to depend upon religious convictions weak or absent in many. We tend to think of these mathematical rules of visual representation as simply correct. Consider, though, the possibility that such attitudes are exactly those predicted by Cusanus for those who have always viewed the world from within Alberti's paradigm.

The point of art cannot be to represent the world as it is, the world itself being quite adequate for that purpose. Any representation of the world contains some element of the unreal, the fantastical, the unnatural, and this is its point. The verisimilitude is an effect used to persuade us of the reality of the fantastical and the unreal. Piero della Francesca painted a contemporary scene with what must have been a shocking realism, in which the incarnate God suffered for our sins. That the image of God is foreign to us while Piero's visual representation of the familiar world through mathematical rules has become unquestioned demonstrates the success of Alberti's vision. That this success has been so total demonstrates, perhaps, the prescience of Cusanus' warnings.

> I do not claim that Alberti is godless. I fear for his soul that he may fall to the sin of pride, of hubris, and in time this may lead men to the unbelief of the Epicureans. When compared against this, the arguments for heresy in Plato are divisions between those who must unite in the shadow of a greater danger. I have heard of the vexation caused to you by the rhetorician and copyist George of Trebizond through his apparent determination to squabble with Theodore of Gaza. The peace of God is lost to him, and with it his reason. We must pity him, and show mercy. I shall tell you an experience of mine with the poor man, in the hope that you may feel that your troubles are a burden I have shared, and so find the strength required by forbearance.

> Five years ago now Trebizond had a house on the Piazza Di San Macuto. It adjoined that of one Giovanni Toscanella, a native son of Rome and a merchant of some standing. George contrived to reach such bad relations with this man that the matter came to violence. I invited Trebizond as a guest into the Vatican palace so that the situation might diffuse. This was three days before I too was set to depart to join the Holy Father in Mantua.
>
> Trebizond, sent home prior to my departure, was set upon by Toscanella's men: it would have gone badly for him had not his son Iacopo likewise arranged a mob in support of his father. George survived by being taken from his horse and hidden in another house, but the violence was such that other lives were lost. I was delayed from my travels while a truce was effected. It is true that on both prior occasions when these two belligerents had gone to court the judgement had gone in George's favour, yet I cannot free myself from the suspicion that another man in his place might have invited less hostility through his manner. May peace find him, for I do not think he will stir one pace to seek it out, much less forgive Plato for the accident of preceding the coming of Christ into the world. He seems quite unable to recognise that, in the writings of the pagans, it is not the text which changes, but rather our reading of it.

In his post as Vicar-General of the Papal States Nicholas was responsible for the temporal rule of Rome given that the Pope was in Mantua. As with Poggio Bracciolini, Cusanus sympathises with Bessarion in the antagonism he is experiencing from George of Trebizond with an example from his own experience. Trebizond's extreme and public confrontations with Toscanella here related should be recollected when reading Trebizond's own letter in this collection with regard to his claims in respect of his interactions with Sigismondo Malatesta.

> To return to the question of Sigismondo Malatesta, as your attempts to communicate with him directly have proven fruitless, might I suggest that you inquire further from his brother, Malatesta Novello of Cesena? While he is of course bound to Sigismondo by blood, they have also vied in competition for their territories. Novello is something more

> of a scholar than his older brother, and has created a library, not merely his own private library, nor one dedicated to the church, but for the commune of Cesena, to be available to the public, with the idea of promoting learning amongst the laity of his polity. We may debate whether he is promoting error amongst those without appropriate clerical training, but there can be no doubt that Novello is a different man from Sigismondo. I expect he would provide an enlightening reply to an inquiry from Your Eminence regarding this matter.

Cusanus ends by recommending to Bessarion Sigismondo's brother Malatesta Novello of Cesena on the basis that Novello is not only a fellow scholar, but also to some degree estranged from Sigismondo. It appears that Bessarion did indeed follow up Cusanus' advice following the death of his friend and colleague, for the chronologically subsequent letter is Novello's reply. As shall be seen, it appears that Bessarion did more than simply write to Novello, first making him a gift by which to encourage his compliance.

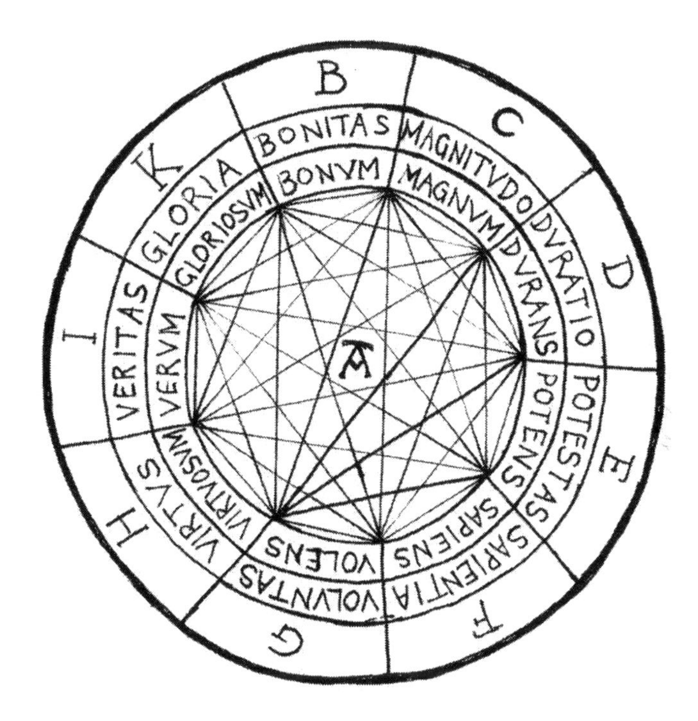

Figure 10: One of the discs encoding the *Ars Magna* of Ramon Llull, sketch by A.B. Cromar

The Letter of Malatesta Novello,

Master of Cesena, to Cardinal Basilios Bessarion, September 1465

Novello chooses to write to Bessarion in Latin. As noted by Poggio Bracciolini, Bessarion had administered Bologna for five years, so his comprehension of Romagnol would certainly be adequate for Novello to have written in his native vernacular had he so desired. His choice of Latin may be a courtesy to Bessarion, but I think it probable that it is also a matter of Novello presenting himself as a scholar.

> Your Eminence does me honour by your generosity in respect of the songbooks: they adorn the meagre collection of codices which I have managed to amass as rubies set among the pebbles of the shore. Your consideration of the character of the recipient in respect of such gifts does not go unnoticed: I have seen that painting by Piero della Francesca which you gave to Federico of Urbino, so fitting to that Prince's love of images and decorations in the new style. I am aware that the death of Holy Father Pius prevented Federico from repaying you with his assistance in your endeavour; alas! in my own case the obstacle is an ailment by which I am besieged and have been quite incapable of freeing myself.

Novello's standing as a scholar is flattered by Bessarion in his gifting him the songbooks he mentions. Several of these may still be seen in the library which Novello's built at Cesena, the reading room of which is preserved in its original fifteenth century form. The songbooks are perhaps thirty inches high and twenty-four wide, with text and musical notation marked in rich colour and large font such that they could be followed by a full choir. They numbered eighteen in Bessarion's original donation, although not all are still held by the *Biblioteca Malatestiana.*

Here is also confirmed the suspicion that the painting mentioned in the letter of Leon Battista Alberti, executed by Piero della Francesca, was a gift of Basilios Bessarion to Federico da Montefeltro for the purpose of encouraging Federico towards joining the crusade against the Turks. Novello notes that, as the songbooks are an apt gift for himself, this painting is an appropriate gift for Federico. This is because it was an image in the new style: as Alberti opined in his comparison of Federico's palace at Urbino with the *Castel Sismondo*, Federico was perhaps more 'modernist' in his tastes than Sigismondo: he was, after all, five years younger. Exactly what was meant by all the details of the enigmatic scene portrayed by Piero della Francesca is probably lost to us forever, but this is an intriguing connection to an intriguing work of art.

Novello also mentions the death of Pope Pius II which had occurred on the 14th of August, only three days after that of Nicholas of Cusa, with his fleet still at anchor in Ancona, still unreconciled with Sigismondo Malatesta. With him died the impetus for crusade against the Turks. He was succeeded by Paul II, author of another of these letters and original recipient of that sent by George Trapezuntius.

> In lieu of more actively aiding you in the matter of my brother, and to assure you of the love I bear you, I shall provide you with my own testimony regarding him from my recollections of our childhood together and the formation of his character; I appeal to your discretion with regard to what I shall divulge here. In respect of Sigismondo as a child, or Gismondo as he was then, I believe that I am uniquely stationed to speak.

It is clear that Bessarion had contacted Novello, and made the gift of the songbooks, with the explicit aim of having Novello assist in persuading Sigismondo to do as Bessarion wanted. Exactly what this entailed is unclear: with the death of Pius II just as his crusade was about to sail across the Adriatic it seems that Bessarion's schemes had rather collapsed. By the time of this letter Sigismondo had returned to Italy: with the loss of momentum on other fronts it is not apparent what else he could reasonably have achieved.

It also seems to be the case that Bessarion continued at this late stage to value personal insight into Sigismondo Malatesta the man. This can only plausibly have been in order better to manipulate him, unless, following the incomprehension expressed by Nicholas of Cusa at Sigismondo's apparent unconcern for the damnation of his soul, Bessarion was struggling to understand why his target was, to a large degree, beyond his ability to control.

> What love there was between Sigismondo and myself has been consumed by the passing of the years. Sigismondo is

not the man his enemies would paint him as, but neither is he a good man. I fear that he was set on a course for Hell long before that puppet-show on the piazzas of Rome. In our youth, however, he did love me well, and was brave and generous in my protection. I shall confess what I know of his sins, that you may yet save him from perdition, if that is your intent and it lies within your power.

I hold that it is best to begin at the beginning. I shall provide you with my own testimony regarding my brother from my recollections of our childhood together and the formation of his character.

I was nine years old when my father Pandolfo died and my brothers and I went to live with our uncle Carlo at RImini. I was then Domenico, and my older brothers were Gismondo, a year my senior and from the same mother, Antonia da Barignano, as well as our half-brother Galeotto Roberto, a further six years older than Gismondo. None of us were born in wedlock; none of us possessed rights to any legacy. Our uncle was then in his fifty-ninth year, married to Elisabetta daughter of Ludovico Gonzaga the Captain of the People at Mantua; a woman of high piety, but destined to remain childless.

You know Carlo Malatesta, like his brother our father, to have been a most capable soldier, ruling Rimini as vicar of the Pope. Both Pandolfo and Carlo, by my own estimation, cultivated all the learning required of princes, not merely those martial talents by which they got their wealth. One difference I perceive now, reflecting on my childish impressions from the vantage-point of age, is that Pandolfo evinced less Christian piety than Carlo. I do not mean to say that my father was in any way anything other a Christian, but Carlo displayed stronger sentiment against the teachings of the ancient pagans. Although the incident occurred more than twenty years before I was born, I believe this was behind Carlo's destruction of the statue of Virgil which had stood in Mantua, which he tore down and cast into the river Mincio. It was not that Carlo was without humanist learning, for, years later, he hosted the Florentine Leonardo Bruni, but something in him rebelled against it, something which I

> believe had to do with his knowledge of his sins and his desire to turn more fully to Christ in repentance.
>
> I argue that this battle fought in the soul of our uncle played out in the different actions of we three, his nephews. Sharing the extreme Christian devotion of our aunt Elisabetta, Galeotto had one sole desire, which was to become a friar of the Franciscans. Among the list of crimes of which Sigismondo was accused by Holy Father Pius was the murder of our older half-brother, but I can tell you, Your Eminence, that in this, as in many others of the charges, the Holy Father was deceived by Sigismondo's enemies. Galeotto did not die at the hand of any man, but made way as did that other Prince Galeotto for Launcelot, being taken to God before the natural span of his life as a result of his own mortification of his flesh, the sinfulness of which he could not endure. He would wear a horsehair girdle. He would flagellate himself daily. He slept on a wooden plank. He had these tendencies in him as a child, but only moved to such extremes following the death of our father Pandolfo.

Novello makes reference to that Galeotto, French Galehaut, of the Grail legend, the companion so devoted that he yields victory in combat, the love of Guinevere, and even his life for the sake of Lancelot.

> Gismondo was far more Pandolfo's son, a learned man, less pious than Carlo. Gismondo loved the examples of the ancients, identifying with such as Scipio Africanus, or Aeneas, but, rather than leave them in their books, he would test himself against their example, whether in the hunt or the joust. Poetry was not for him a written, dead thing: it was for public proclamation as Virgil or Homer would have it. He was, even when young, a great soldier and huntsman, inspirational in both speech and action. But he was impulsive, he could be reckless, and, worse, he was capable of a cruelty which shocked me. I shall share with you an incident I recall from our childhood by which to illustrate this for you.

A quite different incident is quoted in '*Un Condottiere au XVième Siècle*' by Monsieur Yriarte - who makes no mention of this one - in which the boy Gismondo plucks naked a live, captured dove such that it dies of shock, to the horror of Galeotto Roberto. However, in that account Domenico is also complicit in the cruel act.

> We were hunting for deer with horse and hounds, Uncle Carlo, Gismondo and I, and some retainers of the court. We had chased down a stag, and the hounds were worrying it, but it was a full-grown beast bearing a crown of a dozen points by which it held them off. My brother took a lance and spurred his horse forward. The stag feinted, but still Gismondo caught it in the haunch and maimed it, though the lance was wrested from his grasp. The wounded stag flung up its lowered head; the horse reared up as it came on, and threw Gismondo. The stag got all the points of its antlers beneath the chest of the horse coming down and gored it sorely. Stag, horse and rider thus fell all three together, but Gismondo rose and held himself upright for a moment, before drawing his sword and advancing. We others by now had ridden up; Carlo and some retainers dismounted, but I sat in my saddle and observed.
>
> Gismondo approached the stag which was still trying to rise, its antlers caught by the horse's forelegs and rib cage in which some points were still embedded. He deftly thrust, and, piercing the heart, dispatched the stag straight away. Then he turned to his horse, stopped, and looked in the eye which it rolled in its distress. I thought perhaps it was pity which stayed his hand, or otherwise sorrow that a fine steed should have come to such an end, and so I called to him that the horse could not be saved and must be killed. He turned around on hearing me, but rather than sorrow or pity, his face wore a smile. I realised then, the horse having failed him, that it pleased him to see its affliction and the drawing out of its death. Carlo, rather than place blame on a dumb beast, plainly regarded the unfortunate spectacle as Gismondo's doing; coming forward he drove his own blade into the horse's heart. He stared at Gismondo in fury, who silently returned a gaze of calm defiance. This cruelty has never left him, and he has showed it to more than animals in the intervening years. But he has his reasons, which, though I have never told them to any living soul, I shall reveal to you here, Your Eminence.

My assessment of myself is that I am less soldier than Gismondo and less saint than Galeotto; my main interest is learning, to which end I created my library, and then gifted it to the commune of Cesena. I leave it for the betterment of her citizens, so that my legacy might be seen not in marble nor bronze, neither in poems nor encomia, but only in the example of the learning of the people.

Holy Father Martin legitimised my brothers and myself, first Galeotto Roberto and then, in the year 1428, Gismondo and me. This was, as fortune dictated, timely, for Carlo died the following year, and Galeotto became ruler of Rimini. But he was ill-suited to rule, concerned only with Christian piety. To be Lord of Rimini; to have had to marry Margherita, daughter of the House of Este; to be required to consummate that marriage: these things were abhorrent to Galeotto. Within a year forces were sent against him by the Holy Father, with the claim that Carlo had owed lands to the Pontiff. But no such move had been made against Carlo, and I think the Holy Father's reasons were instead that he believed Galeotto incapable of defending his lands, which he held as a vicar of the states of the Holy See, and so Martin felt he must seize them himself before they fell to another. But the Holy Father had reckoned without Gismondo.

A force came, led by our cousin of the Malatesta of Pesaro, also named Carlo as our uncle had been. They moved to surround the town, outnumbering manifold the fighting men within. Gismondo, though still a boy of thirteen years, took to his horse and rode through the camp of the enemy and on to Cesena, where he spoke in the marketplace beseeching the men of that town to come to the aid of Rimini. I watched for his return, and when I saw the dust which rose with the coming of their host I readied the men of Rimini; as Gismondo fell upon our enemies, we threw open our gates and rode out also, trapping our besiegers in disarray between our two forces, and so routed them.

These events did nothing to steer Galeotto Roberto toward worldly concerns, but in a further two years that situation resolved itself when all his bodily mortifications made him so weak that he died of fever, raving in prayer all the while.

As I have said, there was no need for Gismondo to kill him. I think death could not come soon enough for Galeotto Roberto.

He was buried in the church of Saint Francis in Rimini. The people deemed him a Saint, and still come for alms to his tomb. After the funeral Gismondo came to me and told me his wish to divide the realm between us. He was to have Rimini and the south, I Cesena and the north. I thanked him for this honour, but asked him why he did not keep for himself all the lands? After all, Uncle Carlo had held the full realm, and he could surely emulate Carlo.

Gismondo spat. I looked to his face and saw a mask of cold anger. He spoke. "Domenico my brother, I share our lands with you in hope that you might be a new kind of Malatesta, a better man than me or our father Pandolfo, and certainly a better man than the devil Carlo Malatesta."

I was astounded. He looked away from me and went on.

"For these past three years I have defended the rule of our brother Galeotto from those enemies without who would seize it, but I was not able to protect him, or myself, from the enemy within our own family. You, my little brother, I succeeded in protecting, which is why you have not known until today who it was who bears the fault of Galeotto's pitiable death."

"Galeotto was always a more pious Christian than you or I. But his mortification of these last years, since our father Pandolfo died, you well know to have been excessive, and of a different character than before. You have imagined that this was the influence of Elisabetta our aunt, through her example. But now, little brother, you must know why she, like Galeotto, was so constantly in prayer, so consumed by shame. For Carlo used Galeotto as his unwilling Ganymede in the sin of the Sodomites. I believe our aunt knew it all. I do not try to imagine what perversions he may have committed against her person also. And when Galeotto wasted away, in his disgust at himself, in his yearning for death and desperation for Heaven, Carlo turned his foul attentions towards me. This was in the last year of his life. I will feel no shame for his sin against a youth placed in his charge. And I will not suffer a man to wrong me without redress."

"I killed him, Domenico, with slow poison, so that he seemed but a man old and infirm, prey to illness. I have confessed this to no priest, for I ask no pardon for it; no, not of any God, much less of any man who claims to speak for such. It was indeed in my mind that I could protect you, but no part of the burden of his death should be borne by you. I killed him for the wrong he did to me, and would have done so had I no brother to avenge or to protect."

This crime, Your Eminence, is enough to see the soul of Sigismondo wait out eternity in Caina. But by it he saved me from my uncle's libidinous perversions. I have my suspicions that Carlo's sin is one of which my brother has himself been guilty since that time, but I do not know this with certainty. Moreover, Nor do I know whether he would ever have committed it without having been Carlo's victim: it seems to me that there is something in men that they will not turn the other cheek, but must be revenged, even if their revenge is wrought on some new innocent rather than he who wronged them. It may be that Carlo suffered the same sin against him in his youth. It may be, too, that Pius was right to see the sins of the Malatesta passed through the generations of our house, from father to son, on and on. I am sure only that this sin has not touched me, and for that I have to thank my brother Sigismondo.

From that time onward, of course, we ruled from our two separate cities of Rimini and Cesena, and so we began to grow apart. But there were still many occasions on which we came together, and on which I believe I might usefully comment, knowing my brother more closely than others do.

The first of these was a year after the death of Galeotto Roberto, when Sigismund of Luxembourg was crowned Holy Roman Emperor in Rome by Pope Eugene. Passing through Rimini, he knighted Gismondo and me. I took the name Malatesta Novello that I might be that new Malatesta for whom my brother had hoped. The warrior in Gismondo revelled in his knighthood, and he remade his name to

Sigismondo, after the Emperor, and assumed Saint Sigismund as his patron. This defined him, I feel, allowing him to make of himself a man who could overshadow Carlo his uncle, having been knighted not by some minor prince of Italy, but rather the Emperor himself. When he had the Church of Saint Francis in Rimini rebuilt according to the design of Leon Battista Alberti, he commissioned from Piero della Francesca a fresco, hidden in the reliquary, in which Sigismondo is seen kneeling before Saint Sigismund, and the face he had Piero give to the Saint is that of the Emperor.

The year after our knighthoods I married Violante da Montefeltro, a union which has strained our brotherly bond since as that house has been to him the greatest rival. In the same year Sigismondo married Ginevra, daughter of Niccolò d'Este by Parisina who was a daughter of Andrea our uncle who had ruled in Cesena. You will know that Sigismondo married in spite of his prior betrothal to the daughter of the *condottiere* Francesco Bussone, from whom he had accepted a fine steed and a finer suit of armour, the helm all worked in silver; when he broke off the engagement Sigismondo, of course, retained these gifts.

There was no love between Sigismondo and Ginevra. It might be supposed that Sigismondo would feel pity for the girl because her mother, who Niccolò had beheaded for adultery some nine years before, had been our cousin. But Sigismondo married solely for the union with Ferrara; he perhaps approved of Niccolò's treatment of his mother-in-law. Six years later he was accused of poisoning Ginevra, as you know. That is, for the reason which will now be obvious to you, an act of which I believe my brother entirely capable. It merely happens to be the case that he did not do it. No accusations arose at the time; those that were made came years later, from his enemies, and Sigismondo's good relations with the House of Este were in no way harmed by the death of Niccolò's daughter.

Nor did Sigismondo kill his second wife, Polissena, daughter of Francesco Sforza; furthermore, he did not order her to be killed. I do not mean by this that he treated the girl well, for the contempt which he showed her was yet greater than that to which he had subjected Ginevra. He married Polissena in 1441, but within four years his love for the girl Isotta, daughter of the merchant Francesco degli Atti, was being celebrated at his court in poetry and song. A prince will have mistresses, and Sigismondo, Galeotto and I were all born in bastardy, indeed Sigismondo's son Roberto was born to his mistress Vanetta dei Toschi in the year he married Polissena, but my brother humiliated Polissena wilfully. She died after eight years of marriage, her body of plague, but it seemed to me that her spirit was already dead from shame.

You will observe, Your Eminence, that in rejecting the charges made against my brother I do not claim him to be anything other than a great sinner whose soul is surely bound for Hell, unless he sincerely repent and throw himself upon the mercy of Christ and His Church. I am, however, intrigued as to why the specific charges against my brother, that he murdered his first two wives, were made when these are false, while the killing of his uncle has never been mentioned. I will lay out my hypotheses, Your Eminence, and you may then correct my errors and lead me back to the truth.

I speculate that Sigismondo has never been accused of Carlo's murder because to do so would invite the revelation of the sins of Carlo Malatesta who had been the loyal servant and soldier of the Pope. Naturally I do not mean by this that the priests of the Roman Catholic Church would knowingly protect the reputation of a man whose predilection was pederasty. But it did not suit the purposes of Sigismondo's enemies such as Federico da Montefeltro or Alessandro Sforza to make this accusation.

As to why Pius II as Holy Father was so attached, in his accusations against my brother, to listing crimes of a sexual nature, and of the murder of his wives, I fear that here my hypothesis indeed touches upon the character of the former Holy Father as a man. We both know that in his youth Aeneas Piccolomini was a scholar of a liberal disposition. He wrote *The Story Of Two Lovers* and the *Chrysis* in which he portrays priests unable to resist their lustful urges. He fathered more than one bastard. But it seems to me that something changed in him, a few years before he rose to the office of Holy Father; perhaps the change which allowed him to become a man suitable to the apostolic succession. That is of course not for me to say. He appeared, though, to develop a particular and personal distaste for the sexual, and, of the accusations made against my brother, my reading is that it was such on which Pius vented the greater part of his anger.

I expect you will be able to correct me where I err in my surmising, Your Eminence. I hope that my soul is not beyond salvation, though of course that rests on the benefit of clergy. Perhaps it still remains within the power of Christ's Church to bring to repentance and salvation the soul of my brother Sigismondo Pandolfo Malatesta, although Pius who condemned him is now himself in Paradise.

My brother is perceived as having made enemies of all around him out of simple greed when he betrayed Alfonso of Naples in the matter of the Milanese succession, going over to the Florentines while keeping the fee he had been paid. He has never returned this money, and I hold that this is the real crime for which the former Holy Father cast his soul into eternal damnation; that he jeopardised the unity of Italy which had been sought, for which he was excluded from the Peace of Lodi, and which was ever a thorn to the Holy Father, that a Vicar of the Papal territories should be unreconciled with Naples and the Aragonese.

I do not imagine that you will think better of my brother if I tell you the real and secret reason for his great error, but it is nevertheless the truth; we are both men who choose the pains of knowledge over the comforts of ignorance. And the truth is that Sigismondo knew as he chose this path that it would lead him to disaster, but that it was a choice he made for reasons which were, to his mind and heart, noble.

The Florentines have, for decades now, imagined themselves heirs to the republican spirit of ancient Rome, and a great spate of humanist learning has flowed from that town across all Italy and beyond. But in one key way they are wholly different from those our Italian forebears. For while all the arts prosper amongst the Florentines, their native art is commerce. They are merchants who buy with money all their glories. And this includes their soldiers. No *cursus honorum* applies on the Arno: citizenship of their Republic is bought with Florins, not with the mettle of the line of battle.

Sigismondo is a humanist. The example of the pagans is strong for him, and he will fear Hell no more than he will fear any mortal man. He is content that God will do with him as He will, but his mind is its own place, and he would think it better to stand in Hell than to kneel in Heaven. In his respect for the example of the Florentine Republic, Sigismondo chose to aid them against the authority of Naples. He knew that this was not the route to profit. He sacrificed himself that day, and has awaited judgement for it ever since. What, then, did it gain him to return the fee to Naples? As well being hanged for a sheep as a lamb, he kept the money.

It built much of what can be seen of his church in Rimini. There are many who say that he has made of it a pagan temple, and I do not disagree. You will see, from what I have told you, that he rebels both against the sinful hypocrisy of his uncle and the meekness of our brother and aunt in their response to it. The Christian piety by which they turned the other cheek was not for him, and he turned, instead, away from Christ. The sentence which Pius passed on him, which since Pius' death is unlikely to be revoked, was redundant. Sigismondo will not kneel to Christ or His church.

Among the accusations made by Pius against Sigismondo was that of Epicureanism, the repudiation of any existence but the material, that there is neither immortality nor purpose to our lives. The greatest proof of the falsity of this charge is the *Tempio*, and the most persuasive feature of the *Tempio* is the tomb of the scholar Georgios Gemistus, whose bones Sigismondo recovered from Mystras during his campaign in the Morea against the Turk. I believe Gemistus was your own teacher at one time, Your Eminence. This man was not a priest, but a philosopher, known as Pletho for being a new Plato. In his final years he had abandoned all pretence at recognising the teachings of the Church or the revelation of the gospels, following his own mind in his determination of the truth. My brother Sigismondo was not a scholar at heart, Your Eminence, but in this independence of mind he was indeed a kindred spirit of that great philosopher of the Hellenes, a soul beyond the judgement of men or of God. Of whatever else Pletho may stand accused, as with Plato before him, a belief in the death of the soul and the primacy of this base world of appearances cannot reasonably be included. As for Pletho, so for Sigismondo.

Consider the fresco by Piero Della Francesca in the reliquary of his temple. It claims to show Sigismondo kneeling before Saint Sigismund. But the Saint wears the likeness of the Emperor who knighted him, and it is Sigismondo himself who is central, beneath his coat of arms. This piety is not Christian. I believe that Sigismondo has his gods, but that they are Mars and Minerva, Jupiter and Apollo, and they do not require him to kneel. They require him, rather, to emulate the example of the ancients, with the only immortality to which he aspires being renown.

For my part, while my excommunication has been lifted, and I am permitted to retain my position while I live, on my death my lands will revert to the Holy See. I have no heir to whom my rule might have passed. This results from a vow which I made to my wife to father no bastards, which I made recognising that congenital evil inherited through the Malatesta line which Pius identified. But this means that while others may aspire to heaven, the things of this world are all that those of my house may ever hope to have. For this reason I ask you, Cardinal Bessarion, if you might influence our new Holy Father to concede, upon my death, to have my lands revert to Sigismondo my brother who gave them to me freely. I undertake in exchange to assist as I may in persuading my brother to further exertions in service to your cause, once I have thrown off this current illness which assails me.

My own legacy will be my library, which I bequeath not to the Church, nor to another lord or scholar, but to the people of Cesena. More than the particular collected codices, or the building to house them, my legacy is this idea, this public

> library. For the gift of beautiful books, then, I thank you, Cardinal Bessarion.

The marriage of Novello and Violante da Montefeltro produced no children, as was reasonably common: Violante's father Guidantonio had no children with his first wife, Novello's aunt Rengarda; neither Novello's father Pandolfo nor his uncle Carlo fathered children in wedlock, Novello and his brothers being born of Pandolfo's mistresses. Having made his vow to Violante that he would father no bastards, Novello therefore died childless. In this letter it is suggested that Novello chose this because of his belief in the congenital evil of the Malatesta line: whether this is true or was told to Bessarion for effect I am unable to determine.

Novello would never throw off the illness of which he writes, dying of this long illness in November 1465, two months after the date of this letter. Control of his territories reverted to the Pope, now Pius' successor Paul II. While still fractious, the relationship of Sigismondo and Paul was better than with Paul's predecessor: in early 1466 Paul presented Sigismondo with the Golden Rose for his service in the Morea, but in 1467, when Paul would not accede to Sigismondo's requests with regard to lands he formerly held, Sigismondo allegedly plotted to have Paul killed. By early 1468 Sigismondo was once more fighting in the Pope's service. It is unclear what part, if any, Bessarion played in this.

The tone of this account generally fits what is known of the relationship of Malatesta Novello and his brother: militarily they had been both allies and enemies throughout their adult lives, clearly having some distance between them. This difference in character is clear from their different building projects. Both constructed a modern fortress in their respective cities: that of Sigismondo sits within Rimini in clear display to his people, while at Cesena Novello's is set up aloof, looking outward. Their choice of public building projects differentiates them also, Novello providing a public library while Sigismondo chose a temple dedicated to his own glory.

Figure 11: Tomb of Gemistus Pletho, Tempio Malatestiano southern wall, drawing by A.B. Cromar

The Letter of George Trapezuntius,

Of Candia to Pope Paul II, December 1468, forwarded to Cardinal Basilios Bessarion accompanied by the Holy Father's covering letter.

Four centuries before Christ, but a dozen years after the Athenians had swatted their biting gadfly with a fatal hemlock draught, a select group sheltered from the blazing Attic sky in the cricket-chirping, oregano shade of an olive grove aboriginally sacred to Athena, a mile beyond the Dipylon Gate. This was the school of philosophy and dialectic, the Academy of Aristocles Aristonides, known as Plato. Later legend holds that above the door was inscribed "let none but geometers enter here": with no constructed doorway this is apocryphal, but one containing the truth of mathematics as central to their philosophy. That language talked of another world, a world known innately, a purer world of perfect forms.

Five centuries elapsed before Claudius Ptolemy, working in the Greek culture of Roman Alexandria, set down in his mathematical treatise the canonical description of this, our less perfect world, applying mathematics to the ordering of its geocentric cosmos: the planetary spheres and fixed stars; the ecliptic and the equinoxes; their precession and the epicycles; the eclipses of the sun and moon.

Lost to Western Europe, in the twelfth century Gerard of Cremona of the Toledo school translated from an Arabic copy this "greatest" treatise - Greek *megiste*, hence Arabic *al-majiste* - into Latin as the 'Almagest'. Although this and other versions from such sources were error-prone, nevertheless the Ptolemaic universe is recognisably the one in which, for example, the *Paradiso* of Dante's *Commedia* was set.

The *quattrocento* saw Greek versions of the *Almagest* brought to Italy, and Greeks to translate them. One such was George of Trebizond, who produced both a Latin translation, which was a great boon to western scholars, and a full commentary, which was not. The language which George had failed to master was neither Greek nor Latin, but mathematics.

While his surname of Trapezuntius derived from his family's origins in the Empire of Trebizond, he was in fact from Candia, modern Chania, in Crete. This made him a subject of the Venetian Republic, and he came to Venice as a young man. George quickly gained fluency in the Latin language, studying under Vittorino da Feltre (also tutor to Federico da Montefeltro and the children of Poggio Bracciolini). In 1426, at the age of 21, he converted to Catholicism, determining to achieve fame through Latin eloquence.

George appears to have been talented, but a snob, unable to resist denigrating perceived rivals. An early preference for Plato over Aristotle was turned on its head, apparently on reading the *Gorgias*, in which Plato brilliantly critiqued rhetoricians, which Trebizond had now committed himself to be. George's patron, Francesco Barbaro, had said in a letter of 1436 that Trebizond would be peculiarly well suited to confounding the Greeks at the council of Basel. Whatever Trebizond's rhetorical skills, Georgios Gemistus Pletho apparently foiled this expectation. From one who identified so explicitly with Plato this was the ridicule of the *Gorgias* repeated publicly, which George's vanity could not tolerate. So it was that in 1458 he wrote his 'Comparison of the Philosophies of Aristotle and Plato' in response to 'Wherein Aristotle Disagrees with Plato' which Gemistus had written while at the Council. Trebizond's is a work of invective more than philosophy. It is from here that he quotes in this letter his conversation in Florence with Pletho.

While Bessarion and Trebizond had known each other since at least the Council, and Bessarion had been a patron of George's at the Curia, the 'Comparison...' saw the end of any possibility of cordial relations between the two. This was five years after the incident recounted by Bracciolini of their fracas in the chancery which led to Trebizond leaving for Naples, having refused to undertake further translations for Pope Nicholas V. Amongst the last works he had completed was the commentary on Ptolemy's *Almagest*, which was criticised by, amongst others, Bessarion, who then commissioned a more competent version from George von Peuerbach, completed by Johannes Regiomontanus. It was a printed edition of this commentary which, encountered during his studies at Bologna University at the close of the fifteenth century, inspired a young Pole named Nicholas Copernicus to devote his efforts to astronomy.

From the Latin

> Rotting in a sarcophagus on the wall of the Church of Saint Francis in Rimini lies, I contend, a dire threat to Christendom, Your Holiness, as I shall explain. I have learned of the recent death of Sigismondo Pandolfo

> Malatesta, who had ruled in Rimini. This was the man so uniquely lost to sin that your predecessor as Holy Father damned him while he lived, wisely having seen that excommunication from the Church was in his case insufficient.

Sigismondo had died on the 7th of October 1468, at the age of 51, in the *Castel Sismondo,* to be buried in his ornate chapel in the Church of Saint Francis which is also the *Tempio Malatestiano.*

> I met the man last year. This was shortly after your mercy ended my imprisonment in the Castel Sant' Angelo. I thank you again for your wisdom regarding my communications with the Sultan of the Turks. Others, with sight less clear, imagined that I might act in any way contrary to the interests of the Church and your authority as the Vicar of Christ. My endeavours to convert Mehmed II to the Catholic faith were, after all, no more than Holy Father Pius II himself had also assayed.

Trapezuntius stood condemned by his own hand, having written in praise of the Sultan as "King of Kings" in 'On the Truth of the Faith of Christians to the Emir'. Pope Pius II had indeed made the offer to recognise the Sultan Mehmet as eastern emperor if he would accept "the smallest amount of baptismal water", cf. the interception of Matteo de' Pasti mentioned by Vettore Cappello in his letter.

George had warned Mehmet of the need to unite all men under one religion, and demonstrated how Islam and Christianity might be reconciled. It is true that George was basically trying to convert Mehmet through a demonstration of the truth of the Trinity. It is also true that Pius II had attempted exactly the same. Nonetheless when in 1466 Bessarion intercepted further letters in which George expressed the view that Mehmed was King of Kings *by divine right*, declaring an ambition to serve him, Trebizond was only saved from dying in a cell of the Castel Sant' Angelo by the mercy of Pope Paul II.

Paul's clemency seems to have followed from an assessment of Trebizond as an essentially harmless madman. During his imprisonment George had written of Mehmet as "Manuel, a son of Ishmael, descendant of Abraham [...] fulfilment of the prophecies". These ideas had already been laid out in 'On Awesome Things' and

'On the Approach of the Antichrist' where George read these prophecies into the bible, predicting that the conversion of Mehmet would provide a last Christian emperor, a mirror of Constantine the Great as the first, ushering in a final two centuries of peace before the coming of the Antichrist and the last days. As a child Paul had been tutored by George: he may have had a personal affection for him, or he may have known him well enough to dismiss him as incapable of posing a genuine threat. He did, however, send this letter onward to Bessarion, seeing a need for something to be done. We shall see in Paul's own letter what he proposed.

> It was in Rome that I met Sigismondo Malatesta. This was because, as befitted him, he stayed in the house of that scurrilous cur Giovanni Toscanella, which adjoins my own on the Piazza di San Macuto. This was after he, like myself, had returned from the east in the previous year. He had of course been sent as captain of a force sponsored by Your Holiness' native city for the relief of the Morea: you will be aware that he delivered, in military terms, nothing, squandering the forces provided to him, failing even to capture the fortress which stands atop the town of Mystras. He retreated and thereafter failed to engage the enemy.

For Giovanni Toscanella cf. the account by Nicholas Cusanus of the dispute between the two men in his second letter here included, that of 1464.

Sigismondo captured the town of Mystras, but failed to take the high crusader fortress which caps it, cf. my notes to the letter of Thomas Palaiologos.

> I have learned, however, that Sigismondo had brought back to Italy something which, while it may appear to others a trivial thing, I hold to be of the highest significance and the gravest danger to Christendom. For at Mystras he unearthed the bones of Georgios Gemistus, known as Pletho, and these he brought back to Italian soil, interring them in the pagan temple he has made of the church of Saint Francis at Rimini. This Pletho denied Christ, by my own witness, as I shall recount for you. Creating of his corpse an invert reliquary was an act of blasphemy and necromancy, yet I hold that Sigismondo was no magician: not for his goodness, of which he had none, but that he was not sufficiently a

> scholar. How and why should a man of such little learning, of such low character, as Sigismondo Malatesta, Your Holiness, have conceived such a plan? Must it not surely be that in this we glimpse the hidden hand of some other, some more learned one guiding Malatesta, some follower of Pletho, a man of no small influence?

Sigismondo buried Gemistus in one of the sarcophagi set in the arches on the side wall of the Tempio Malatestiano, "so that the great Teacher may be among free men". Trapezuntius clearly attempts to implicates Bessarion. Is this simply his lifelong resentment arising from the matters described above?

> I have written much already on the dangers posed by the teachings of Plato to the Christian soul. There are those who will argue that, like his pupil Aristotle, he was a great thinker amongst the pagans before men had the benefit of Christ's gospel to lead them in truth, and that, as the scholars of the church have reconciled the philosophy of Aristotle with Christian doctrine, so too the writings of Plato have value for our comprehension of God's creation. Here they are in error, and have been led to this by that general fascination with the ancients which now prevails, a pestilence cultivated amongst the Florentines. For while in Aristotle we find the doctrines of the immortality of the soul, of creation from nothing, and of one God, although allowing for three persons, in Plato we find instead the doctrine of the existence of the soul before birth, of creation from pre-existing matter, and of a demiurge with a hierarchy of lesser gods below him. You will be aware that all these matters I have already discussed in greater length in my 'Comparison of the Philosophies of Aristotle and Plato'.
>
> That work I wrote in response to 'Wherein Aristotle Disagrees with Plato', which itself was written by Gemistus Pletho while he was in Florence accompanying the representatives of the Greeks at the Council of the Church there. There are those in Italy who would defend Pletho, perhaps out of loyalty to a former teacher; indeed his presence in Florence at that time led to a flowering of interest, both in that city, and then in all Italy, in the ancient knowledge preserved by the Greeks, much of which, of

> course, is instructive and ennobling. I have myself contributed plentifully to the translation into Latin of many such works, and this, moreover, since long before that visit of Pletho to Italy. It is noteworthy, however, how little attention the actual content of that text of Pletho has received from scholars in Italy. In the Greek world it was quickly countered by Georgios Scholarios, he who became Patriarch of Constantinople after she fell to the Turk. Scholarios knew Pletho well, and saw clearly the heresy in his words and the paganism in his soul.

That Pletho was, in late life, openly pagan is undoubted. His unfinished 'Book of Laws' is unambiguous, discussing not only the old Greek polytheism, but the doctrines of Pythagoras and Plato together with syncretic discussion of Zoroaster and his creed. One manuscript, at the point where Pletho breaks mid-sentence, includes "The rest is to seek, though never to be found; for they say it was destroyed by Scholarios."

> There are those who accuse me of slander against a great scholar, that I am ignorant of Pletho's understanding of philosophy. But the man stands accused out of his own mouth. For I met Pletho at that time, in Florence, where he told me that soon there would be one and the same religion throughout the world. At a Council for the reunification of Christianity, and from a fellow Greek all too aware of the dire threat to the Eastern Empire from the Moslem Turks, this seemed, on the face of it, a reasonable proposition. Indeed, all men must surely see it as the great pressing issue of our age, with the central duty of all Christians being to strive our utmost to see that the victorious religion is Christianity under the authority of Christ's appointed, the Bishop of Rome. However, when I asked Pletho whether the religion to be established across all the world, from Ceylon to Britain, would be Christ's or Muhammad's, he answered "Neither. Rather it will not differ from paganism." Shocked by these words, I have always hated and feared him as a poisonous viper and infidel sorcerer.
>
> Your Holiness, I have been arguing this issue all my life. Though a Greek, I was born under the rule of the Most Serene Republic, and had come to Italy and converted to the

> Latin Church before I had the honour to be Your Holiness' teacher. It is well known that it was I who wrote the letter for Holy Father Eugene IV to the Emperor John Palaeologus ahead of the Council for unification, urging him to sail for Italy on the Papal ships for Italy rather than those of the Council, for I could see the overwhelming importance of the unity of Christianity and Christendom under the authority of the Holy Father. Yet now I find my loyalty challenged by those who were at that time not even of the Catholic Church, and who had come under the influence of Platonism as propagated by that new Plato, Georgios Gemistus Pletho.
>
> Depraved Platonic hedonism corrupted the Roman Empire, and in the end brought it to ruin. At the same time the Platonists had a hand in all the heresies which beset the early church. Thereafter a new threat to Christendom has arisen in the form of the teachings and followers of Muhammad, although this second Plato has purged from his instruction the perversions of the first, and moreover has added practical rules of conduct. Consequently, after the degenerate philosophy of the first Plato had enervated Byzantium from within, the devotees of the more astute second have conquered her from without. Then a third Plato appeared, more sensible than the first and more learned than the second: Gemistus Pletho, apostle of a revived paganism. His clever books and ideas are now spreading in Europe. If unchecked, they will undermine our Latin Christianity.

When George writes of "depraved Platonic hedonism" corrupting the Roman Empire, and having "a hand in all the heresies which beset the early church" it should be understood that these had very little to do with anything written in the 4th century BC, but referred to Plotinus, Proclus, and the tradition we today give the name 'Neoplatonism'. The very fact that the Council of Nicaea was deemed necessary attests to the heterogeneity of belief systems within the Empire and beyond. The heresies of Arius, Nestorius and Eutyches appear as cavillous hair-splitting when set against the world-denying tenets of Gnosticism, which deemed the God of Abraham a deluded or evil *demiurge*. This concept, and the greater and more fundamental *Monad* from which the demiurge emanated, are

Platonic ideas preserved by Neoplatonism. It is these multiple levels of divinity to which George of Trebizond refers above as "a demiurge with a hierarchy of lesser gods below him", to be condemned as incompatible with Christianity.

> It may seem that, Pletho being dead, this threat has faded. Yet now Theodore of Gaza, and others like him, disseminate a corrupted understanding of Aristotle, denying the value of older translations, and thereby seeking to bring to naught the work of the Angelic Doctor Thomas Aquinas and all the scholastic tradition of the Church. From philosophy these Platonists will proceed to the demolition of Christian theology which is buttressed by that philosophy. I therefore call upon the Latin clergy, indeed on all who honour the Saviour, to do their duty: if they do not, I fear that a fourth Plato will come, overpassing the previous three in spreading the creed of hedonism, and all Christendom will lower its head to the pupil of Pletho. You can be only too aware of the truth of my words, your Holiness, given that Bartolomeo Platina and Filippo Buonaccorsi, known as Callimachus, Platonists both, are, as I write, held in the Castel Sant' Angelo for the crime of plotting against your life. You may also know that I was able, by means of my correct interpretation of scripture through ancient scholarship, to warn Nicholas V, in his sixth year as Pontiff, of the plot against his life by Stefano Porcari. This provides evidence of the veracity of both my intent and my competence in the protection of the holders of your highest of worldly offices.

While it is not inaccurate to describe both Bartolomeo Platina and Filippo Buonaccorsi as Platonists, it is misleading to attribute their plot against the life of the Pontiff to this cause. Rather they were humanists whose employment in the Curia had depended on the patronage of Pius II, and ended with the accession of Paul, whose lack of enthusiasm for humanism is evinced in his own letter.

On the evidence of a letter of Leon Battista Alberti, Trapezuntius did indeed attempt to warn Nicholas of the plot of Stefano Porcari, having learned of it from a human rather than divine source. Alberti's account notes Bessarion as having been instrumental in actually persuading Nicholas to investigate and uncover the plot.

In like wise I have published 'On Awesome Things', wherein I lay out my interpretations pertaining to our place in the timeline of creation. The Turks and the Mamelukes come from the desert as the sons of Ishmael to sweep away the empires of Greece and Rome. As David foretold in the thirty-second verse of Psalm 67 "Ethiopia will stretch her hand out to God". What does this mean?

Constantinople has fallen, and has now endured fifteen years under Moslem rule. My ancestral fatherland of Trebizond was lost seven years ago. To date the maritime empire of the Most Serene Republic holds my homeland, but other islands of the Greeks have passed from Venetian to Turkish rule. Without the Byzantine bulwark Europe stands open to invasion. It is thus imperative to restore Constantinople to Christian rule, your Holiness, although there are several ways in which this might be brought about. At Mantua, some nine years ago, Holy Father Pius endeavoured to rouse the princes of Christendom in crusade: he had little success, undermined as he was by the Florentines who recommended that he allow the Turks and the Venetians to wear each other out in warfare. I appeal to you as a Venetian, as well as the Vicar of Christ, to consider where in Italy the pagan teachings of Pletho were first promulgated under the guise of humane learning. And so I have tried to continue the other path followed by Holy Father Pius, who looked to the conversion of Mehmed II, and offered to recognise him as Emperor of the East if he would accept even the smallest amount of baptismal water.

I published my treatise 'On the Approach of the Antichrist' nearly three decades ago, following the arrival of the Copts from Ethiopia at the Council of Florence, at the same time that Gemistus Pletho was introducing his pagan Platonism to Italy. The portents surround us, Your Holiness: ancient prophecies are coming to fulfilment. I have possession of two blessed relics brought from Antioch, a golden amulet of sacred glyphs, and an ancient speculum of polished bronze; I have, alongside these, no small expertise of their employment in the scholarly art of scrying, of determining the divine will. I am amanuensis to the Fates. I beseech you

> to heed me, Your Holiness: I believe that we are entering the final two centuries before the breaking of the Eastern Gates; the release of Gog and Magog; the reign of the Antichrist.

Such practises as scrying were not uncommon amongst the clergy, entertained even by Popes on occasion. The inquisition might, of course, become involved in consequence.

> Many will say that these are merely the ravings of a madman. But beware, be attentive to who it is that urges you so, I beg you, Your Holiness. For I spoke to Sigismondo Malatesta when he stayed at the house of Giovanni Toscanella, still hoping that he might not be beyond repentance. I told him that unless he threw out of his city that pagan Apollo who lives in the corpse of Gemistus, some evil would befall him. He promised to do it. He left it undone. Sickness then brought him to the brink of death while still in Rome. He sent for me the hour that he was stricken, so that through the vain predictions of the astrologers I might tell him what would happen to him. Putting my trust in God, I sent the message that in eight days he would be well. After the prophecy came true, I told him that the disease had struck him because he retained in his home the unholy corpse of Gemistus. He promised again that as soon as he returned to Rimini he would cast it into the sea. He returned to Rimini. Again he left it undone. Again he became ill. Before I learned about this, he died, already damned.

Note Trapezuntius' strategy here, of decrying astrology as vain, in contrast to his own prophetic powers which are divinely inspired.

> And so I hope I have made clear, your Holiness, why I attach such importance to the death of this *condottiere*. Though it seems such a little thing, yet it touches upon matters of the greatest moment, that a man of such martial talents should arrange to be sent to the Morea, at Venetian expense, but then achieve no military gain; that a man uniquely canonised into Hell while alive, having laughed at excommunication, should use that expedition only to retrieve the corpse of the pagan heretic Pletho and bury him in consecrated ground upon the shores of Italy; that a man so far from learning, driven by the lusts of fornication and of violence, should have conceived of such a scheme, guided,

> surely, by one more learned and more a disciple to Pletho; that my foretelling to Sigismondo Malatesta of his own death, and the demonstration of my accuracy in the matter, would not make him take one step to undo the urgent jeopardy of his soul. Be very clear, I beg of you, your Holiness: in the life, the death, and the assured damnation of Sigismondo Pandolfo Malatesta I see nothing less than the clandestine intrigues of the Antichrist.

Again Trapezuntius' "one more learned and more a disciple to Pletho" is aimed at Bessarion.

By the time George was writing his letter in 1468 the Florentine Platonic Academy mentioned by Poggio Bracciolini and inspired by Georgios Gemistus Pletho had been established for six years: Cosimo de' Medici had lived to see it, but was dead two years later. He entrusted its oversight to the humanist Marsilio Ficino, and over the next thirty years the works of Plato, as well as Plotinus and other Neoplatonists, were translated from Greek into Latin. In addition to these philosophies Ficino also developed, from his translated ancient texts, a great enthusiasm for astrology and for the teachings attributed to Hermes Trismegistus. Having taken Holy Orders several years previously, he survived the inevitable accusations of heresy.

Against this background is no surprise to find George of Trebizond displaying in this letter what may to us appear a jumble of styles of thought. He might, in his apocalyptic warnings and claims to precognition, strike us as having a ridiculous predisposition to pseudoscience, obscuring the demarcation of scholarly investigation into the workings of creation and the practise of heretical magic. Though he distances himself from the astrologers in his account of predicting Sigismondo's recovery from illness, he has no qualms about claiming predictive powers, indeed confessing his use of magical paraphernalia in the practise of scrying as "amanuensis to the fates". Three points should be borne in mind before we pass our haughty judgements on him, however.

Firstly, the astrologers are still with us, as are those species of Christians who live each day in anticipation of the imminent apocalypse. We have even invented new pseudosciences and new faiths to complement these more venerable traditions: we should be wary of congratulating ourselves for any reduction in our susceptibility to irrationality.

Secondly, the rational scientific progress by which we deem ourselves guided has delivered us into the recent murderous destruction of much of European civilization. If this is rationality its price is too high.

Thirdly, Trapezuntius was a man of his time. We have seen in the first letter of Nicholas of Cusa the beliefs Pope Pius II appears to have held with regard to the reality of Hell, demons, and witches. This speaks to the diverse intellectual currents of the time: further commentary on these issues, on George himself, this letter, and its place in the collection I leave to the commentary on the letter of Pope Paul II.

Figure 12: From the fortress above Mystra towards Sparta and the vale of Eurotas hidden by morning mist, sketch by A.B. Cromar

The Letter of Pope Paul II,

The Letter of Pope Paul II To Cardinal Basilios Bessarion, December 1468

Pope Paul II, who had been Pietro Barbo, a Venetian and nephew of Pope Eugene IV, succeeded Pius II in August 1464. In conclave the Cardinals bound him with several conditions, restricting his travel, requiring him to support crusade &c. History has viewed him as vain with regard to his appearance and devoid of intellectual or spiritual interests, indeed it was just this lack of personal conviction for which he was elected.

From the Ecclesiastical Latin:

> Oblivion in the river of Time is a sentence more elegant than death, Cardinal Bessarion, and more fitting to the matter at hand. I do not write to you as the Servant of the Servants of God, but, rather, privately and in confidence; were this correspondence to become public it would not be advantageous to either of us. The same may be said of the other letter which I have enclosed, which I received from George of Trebizond. You will recognise the confidence which I invest in you by sharing it.
>
> That poor man is quite out of his humour; an excess of yellow bile I suppose, but I am no physician. Upon reading his letter you will understand why I must see his arguments quashed. I believe that some years ago you composed your refutation to his attacks upon Plato, which you then declined to publish due to your commendable restraint and love of peace. Might I suggest that the time to publish is now upon you, Your Eminence? The man has given many years of learned service to the pontifical court; it pains me to detain him further in the Castel Sant' Angelo, but he seems set on a treasonous course of negotiation with the Sultan. In order that his argument be revealed for the madness it is, I therefore suggest that now is the time for a public demonstration of his error with regard to Plato. You know well that I have little interest in the arguments of pagans made before Christ's truth was revealed to man, however wise they may be; I leave this matter in your capable hands.

According to the Hippocratic theory of the humours, unwarranted aggression was explained as a consequence of an excess of yellow bile, or 'choler'.

For Trapezuntius' dealings with Sultan Mehmet see also his own letter and the commentary thereon.

Trapezuntius having written 'Comparison of the Philosophies of Aristotle and Plato' against Pletho's 'On the Differences of Aristotle from Plato', Bessarion had composed his 'Against the Slanderer of Plato' in response in 1459. He did not, however, publish at that time. Here we see Paul urging Bessarion to do so after a decade of restraint, with the aim of discrediting Trebizond. Bessarion's book was not published by the manual copyists of the *Curia* such as Poggio Bracciolini or George of Trebizond: instead it was the first book to be printed in Rome using a press established by Bessarion himself the previous year.

> I know that I am asking you to act against a fellow Hellene, who shares your understandable passion for rousing the western princes against the Turk for the relief of our Christians brothers who suffer beneath the Sultan's oppressive burden. I trust that you see also that your compatriot's schemes in this regard can do only harm to your just cause. I know that I do not demonstrate as much overt action in support of your goal as you might wish, but I would ask firstly that you have faith that your cause is not forgotten, and secondly that you have patience in working steadily towards your end.

The use of the term Hellene is striking, although ambiguous. While Pletho and some others had used the term to identify all those within the Greek heritage of the east, both ancient and contemporary, it generally bore connotations of pagan antiquity which Pletho was not minded to refute. It is not clear whether Paul here intends to slight Bessarion as part of a general strategy throughout this letter of asserting and displaying authority.

> We have a great burden which we carry, passed to us from Christ through Peter and the Apostolic succession. We hold the keys to the kingdom of heaven for all those who live in the body of the Church Militant. Our first concern must be for those who profess the Catholic faith. We must try to lead

> them in righteousness; in order to accomplish this, the Church must have power. It must be united. It must have the resources necessary to its mission. For outside the Church there can be no salvation. Wycliffe and Hus thought that men can appeal to Christ directly, that true goodness comes from making the personal choice to follow the commandments of Christ, and so there is no need for the temporal power of the Church. You and I, dear Bessarion, know better. The masses need our intercession, they need our leadership, they need our authority to cleanse them of their sin. This burden is too heavy for them to bear without us.
>
> It may be that, from time to time, in order that we may save the flock, a single sheep must be sacrificed. I know, Bessarion, that you understand these things, and I do not condemn them. For was it not necessary to Christ's sacrifice for us that Judas Iscariot commit the greatest of all human sins, and be damned to the utmost depths of the inferno, beside only Satan? Without that damnation no other soul may enter paradise. Of course we would have rejoiced had Malatesta come to repentance before he died, and would have welcomed him back into the body of the Church. It was not to be.

Paul reveals himself as a believer in the need for a unified and powerful church for the sake of mankind: having taken over from Christ, through the apostolic succession, as the vehicle for salvation, he has a personal duty as Pope to maximise the number of fallible human beings he can save from perdition, as they are unable to save themselves. In a pragmatic inversion of Jesus' parable of the lost sheep (Matthew 18:12-14, Luke 15:3-7) Paul accepts the need to abandon an individual human soul to damnation in order to save others: he justifies this with the claim that the divine plan of Jesus' sacrifice required his betrayal by Judas Iscariot, whose damnation was therefore the price of salvation being available to Christians at all.

Moreover, Paul makes it clear that he is aware that Bessarion has arranged precisely this for Sigismondo Malatesta: here we have explicit evidence that Pius II's canonisation into Hell of Sigismondo Malatesta was Bessarion's scheme all along, a single human soul sacrificed in the cause of Constantinople. Did the passing mention by

Poggio Bracciolini of his dedicating *On the Misery of the Human Condition* to Sigismondo suggest to Bessarion the identity of his victim? What did Niccolò Perotti know: in this light what might we make of Perotti analogising Sigismondo with Christ? Does Piero della Francesca's *Flagellation of Christ* demonstrate that he, Leon Battista Alberti and Federico da Montefeltro were all involved as well? Was Nicholas of Cusa duped, or complicit? And, for that matter, how do the otherwise apparently demented warnings of George of Trebizond appear in this light?

> You are aware that I am bound by the terms of the conclave to prosecute the war against the Turks. You know also that I choose caution. No Christian believes more firmly than me in the justice and virtue of the cause of Constantinople. But it is not enough to try: we must succeed. Unlike the campaign in the Morea of Vettore Cappello and that Malatesta who was made your puppet; unlike the campaign of Skanderbeg the Albanian which followed it. They have come to naught. I choose the long game.
>
> I shall create the Cardinals preferred by the Kings of Europe, that they become the more bound to the Church. Furthermore, I give you leave to approach the other western princes most likely to support further crusade. Again, I ask you to move patiently. I need not ask you to act with tact and good judgement, for I am unaware of when you have done otherwise; but George of Trebizond has gone ahead of you to the Courts of Hungary and Austria equipped with neither of these virtues.

Paul had a means of resisting the control of those who had thought to constrain him, which was to create new cardinals without consultation, or publishing the names of those appointed, who were supportive of him and his ambitions. As he says these were the preferred candidates of the various kings whose support Paul desired: while superficially appearing shallow and impotent, Paul was able covertly to advance his own agenda. It is this cunning, clandestine and, after all, Venetian politician whose letter this is.

> I shall support your suggestion that Sophia of the house of Palaiologos be married to Ivan, King of the Russians, upon your assurances that she is now committed to our Catholic faith. We must arrange a first ceremony in Rome, under our

> auspices, where she be confirmed in that union according to the rites of our Church. We cannot, I think, expect Ivan himself, or his people, to be immediately brought into communion with Rome. It will, though, be a start, and may, as you suggest, bring the Russians into the brotherhood of powers to whom we may look for support in crusade for the sake of Constantinople. I shall leave the matter with you, as the girl's protector, to progress it further.

Sophia Palaiologina was daughter of Thomas Palaiologos, both of whom authored letters of this collection. Two alternative marriages were proposed by Pope Paul II for Sophia before the one here discussed. The first, to James II of Cyprus, was declined. In the second case the two were betrothed but the marriage never took place. We may conjecture that the reason for this was Bessarion's preference for the marriage to Ivan III of Russia: for Paul the motivation for finding her a suitor would have been primarily to take her off his hands as she was being kept at the expense of the Vatican; Bessarion's motivations would have included a significant requirement to advance the cause of Constantinople. The Rus were at this time a people both small and remote, but Ivan was belligerent and expanding his power.

With the death of Sigismondo Malatesta, Bessarion's scheme to use Sigismondo for his own purposes was over. As we have seen, Piero della Francesca's painting of the Flagellation of Christ may represent an attempt to persuade Sigismondo's rival *condottiere*, Federico da Montefeltro, to Bessarion's cause, although the crusade of Pius II had petered out upon his death, and the new Pope, as we see in this letter, pursuing the matter more circumspectly. The marriage of Sophia Palaiologina becomes Bessarion's next gambit.

Returning to George of Trebizond, who has been rather dismissed as a lunatic, it may be appropriate to re-examine the situation. Certainly he seems to have been arrogant, abrasive and impetuous beyond reason. But it is also the case that George wrote his letter to the Pope warning of a conspiracy centred on Cardinal Bessarion, and we have his letter in this collection precisely because the Pope conspired with Bessarion to silence George. This was not done crudely, such as by prolonging his imprisonment in the Castel Sant' Angelo, but by portraying his views as those of a lunatic, and this is the view of him which has come down to us.

Doubtless George's anti-Platonism appears excessive today. But he was also warning of the insidious danger of ideas which were new to the Catholic west being accepted without due consideration of their implications: that these could threaten the authority of the Latin church and spread traumatic religious warfare throughout Europe. The unfolding of the Reformation and Counter-Reformation over the subsequent three centuries, and the challenge to Christianity of the Enlightenment which followed, suggest that he may have had a point.

It will doubtless be objected that this is not exactly what he described. To point out that precise prediction of the future is a skill denied to mankind would be trite, but it is also the case that George of Trebizond was following different rules in his use of language than would be expected today. If his objection to Plato related to George's identification as a rhetorician as opposed to a philosopher, what might we expect from him? A focus less on the strict logic and reasonableness of what he writes, and more impassioned and florid claims and allegations. And what do we have but this?

It is worth noting that George was introduced in these letters by Poggio Bracciolini's account of their altercation in the chancery of the Vatican, when George was portrayed as mendacious, disrespectful and violent. But this comes from the writer who suggested that Lorenzo Valla should be stabbed for his views on philology, drawing a response from Niccolò Perotti of hiring an assassin. George may have been an extreme example, but he was of a type with these his peers: to judge his language and behaviour against our modern norms is unfair and anachronistic.

This touches upon a more general point about our judgements in respect of historical characters, and the biases we hold with regard to them. By this I mean the habit of regarding history as the path of inevitable progress from past ignorance to contemporary understanding. This fails to recognise that, even if history might legitimately be characterised as linear, this itself would mean that, by comparison with some enlightened future, we now actually stumble forward in woeful ignorance.

We judge favourably men such as Leon Battista Alberti: if Alberti is too obscure, the more celebrated Leonardo da Vinci might be substituted. Such are seen as links in the chain which proceeds through Galileo, Descartes, and Newton to bestow science and rationalism upon the world. Not only the likes of George of Trebizond, but also Nicholas of Cusa suffer in comparison. Yet our contemporary world is filled with doubt as the certainties of scientific progress are challenged, in a manner reminiscent of Cusanus' challenges to Alberti's fixed viewpoint. Moreover, anyone minded to regard George of Trebizond as foolish for holding views which should today indeed appear deranged would do well to recognise that Isaac Newton, a man of indisputable, towering mathematical and scientific genius, undertook considerable alchemical research in search of both the Philosopher's Stone and the Elixir of Life fully two centuries later.

Should we perhaps be less quick to dismiss George of Trebizond simply as the madman he has been painted, but consider the perspective from which we have been invited to view him, and try to be more charitable in our judgement. Was his greatest error, perhaps, to attempt to expose a conspiracy without recognising, in his naïvety, how deep it actually went?

Figure 13: Medal of Isotta degli Atti, drawing by A.B. Cromar

The Letter of Isotta degli Atti,

Regent of Rimini and widow of Sigismondo Pandolfo Malatesta, to Cardinal Basilios Bessarion, January 1470

Isotta was at this time ruling Rimini: following Sigismondo's death in 1468 this was initially as regent to Sigismondo's son Sallustio, but when Sallustio died in 1469 Isotta continued to rule in her own right, a testament to her competence and strength of character.

The letter is written not in Latin, nor in Isotta's native Romagnol, but in literary Florentine, the language of Dante, Petrarch and Boccaccio. Quite why she should have chosen to do this is not immediately apparent. It might be seen as a slight against Bessarion as a non-Italian, or a strategy to choose a language of which Isotta's mastery exceeded the Cardinal's.

Isotta commences her letter thus:

> Dead; he is dead now, Your Eminence. I have fancied myself Cleopatra, bare-breasted to the serpent. In the derelict hours of a dozen dozen nights have dreamed myself as Portia, that I might breakfast on embers. He is dead now, and I loved him.

The death of Cleopatra from the asp delivered hidden in a fruit-basket, as related by Plutarch in his *Life of Anthony*, will be, I think, familiar to all. Portia here is the wife of Marcus Junius Brutus, reputed, on learning of his suicide, to have died by consuming hot coals. She was the daughter of the Younger Cato, for which note Isotta's further reference below. The tone is, to the modern reader, histrionic, but such a weight of classical references was not atypical in her time, and appears to constitute a strategy on Isotta's part of displaying her erudition to the Cardinal. She continues:

> I have roused myself in spite, saying "Know that I do not implore mercy from you, Aeneas Piccolomini, or God either, my Malatesta damned to the inferno, certainly." I determined to poison myself, thinking "Rather to stay there with him below I shall haste, like another Francesca to be with her better Paulo, or Orpheus who, once having looked, turns back to be forever with Euridice, a man sufficient for me as

> my god, and he only I shall worship, my personal Christ, throughout eternity."

Note here that Isotta must address Aeneas Piccolomini posthumously given that Sigismondo outlived him, and also that she refuses to recognise him by his papal name. Her literary allusions continue with Francesco and Paulo Malatesta, perhaps rather unavoidably given that this comparison with Sigismondo's damnation was made by Pius himself. A more Hellenistic parallel of a pair of doomed lovers in the underworld is then introduced, specifically Orpheus and Eurydice, with perhaps connotations of the Orphic mystery-cult: see below for the image of the soul-egg.

> And yet I write to you, being on the hither side of the grave. I find myself no daughter of kings or Catos nobly to cast aside my life in mourning. Shall I rather live all the years of Ishmael, life-weary, bereft of kin and household? In contrite fear I write to you this letter; I offer you my human soul, this egg, Bessarion, Cardinal of the true Church of Christ. I repent my error.

Isotta regrets that she finds herself lacking the fortitude for defiant suicide necessary to join Sigismondo in damnation, confessing her fear and repentance to the Cardinal. Ishmael is an odd comparison for her to make regarding longevity, his one hundred and thirty-seven years being, if anything, remarkably short by the standards of the Biblical patriarchs: the lifespan of Abraham his father was longer by thirty-eight years, for example. Isotta may choose him for as a paradigm of the outcast, but the number of the years of his lifespan may also be important to her for the hidden purpose which I shall discuss separately.

The reference to her soul as an egg perhaps follows the Orphic tradition hinted at with the prior mention of that son of the muse Calliope. The incongruity of such an obviously pagan reference amidst an apparent confession of Christian faith is glaring and, I think, significant; again, however, I leave further discussion for elsewhere.

> I had seen in Sigismondo Pandolfo Malatesta, who was my husband, my prince of refinement and wealth, the god Apollo, shining as the sun which numbers all the year's days. I see now this was indeed he who flayed the living satyr for a

> tune, and slew the blameless brood of Amphion in vengeance for a mother's foolish boast; the one who raped the nymphs and princesses, and fornicated with every Muse; who cursed the chaste Cassandra to speak truth in hendecasyllabic verse, forever disbelieved.

Isotta now offers two contrasting views of Apollo to illustrate her change of heart with regard to Sigismondo. She had adored him as the youthful, virile sun god. Now she recognises this is the same one "who flayed the living satyr for a tune": when the satyr Marsyas challenged Apollo to a contest of music and subsequently lost, Apollo's punishment was to skin him alive. Apollo also, together with his sister Artemis, "slew the blameless brood" of Amphion and his wife Niobe following Niobe's boast of having fourteen children compared to the mere two of Leto, mother to Apollo and Artemis.

As with Sigismondo, Apollo also had many sexual dalliances, some forceful. Isotta mentions Cassandra, who, according to the tragedians Aeschylus and Euripides, was not raped but cursed always to be disbelieved for rejecting Apollo's advances. Note, though, that 'hendecasyllabic' appears erroneous, appropriate in the Greek to Aeolic verse rather than tragedy.

> I have been led astray by love, Cardinal Bessarion. I have been the plaything of Venus and the mark of Eros. The dart I have now removed, but I should be a fool to expect that I shall live all three hundred and forty days remaining in this year. Sallustio, named as Sigismondo's heir, vies with his brother Roberto for power, and I may yet drink the poison previously spurned. I can at least hope to be laid to rest in my chapel in the Church of Saint Francis, commissioned from Messers Matteo de' Pasti and Leon Battista Alberti to the glory of God. I had the honour to meet Messer Alberti, a most impressive man, whose knowledge spans, it seems, all creation. He taught me a trick of writing on an egg which is then hard boiled, the ink of vinegar and alum washed from the shell. This leaves the secreted script, written in unknown signs, confession, oath, curse or instruction as it may be, unseen beneath, such that you might crack, might peel, might read this message found staining the white to black at some time thereafter. But I fear Hell, Cardinal Bessarion, and think how sighs, laments and high wailing greeted the

> Florentine, passing through that dark gate into the city of dreadful night three hundred and thirty verses into his journey to the utmost depths.

The second letter of Nicholas Cusanus notes Leon Battista Alberti's interest in cryptography, although the particular trick described was previously attested only from the following century.

Dante and Virgil's entry to Dis, at the start of *Inferno,* Canto III, occurs less than three hundred verses into the poem. It is difficult to dismiss this as error on Isotta's part given a sufficient familiarity with literary Florentine for her to have composed this letter in that language.

> I was a child when first I met Sigismondo. He was a guest in my father's house as he built the *Castel Sismondo*. All the weeks of one year our Prince stayed with us. I was headstrong and proud, and loathed the mere wealth which followed from my father's honest trade. I had another conception of myself. I wanted in a husband a man who set glory in the vanguard, with wealth following obediently in its train; a man of the old sort, with learning and courtly taste, but with the martial virtues foremost. I wanted to be wed to no merchant haggling and bluffing in the marketplace like those who live by counting the number of the cards of the *Tarocco Bolognese*, aspiring to buy prestige with gold. Though it be the treasury of Croesus, the dreams which it might buy seemed small to me, like the ladies of the Florentines in their silks and vair, who dream of nothing finer than a room with a view of the Arno, and whose minds only connect a man's virtue with his purse. Please believe that I do not forget the number of your years, Your Eminence, when I recount the foolishness of my youth, but I must confess it all.

Isotta was daughter to Francesco degli Atti, a wealthy merchant of Rimini. The substantial family home in the town was near the site of Sigismondo's stronghold, and Sigismondo is indeed recorded as having stayed at the Atti house during construction of the fortress.

The *Tarocco Bolognese* or 'Bolognese Tarot', was the initial European precursor of our playing-cards, used additionally in the practise of cartomancy as beloved of those predators upon the superstitions of the credulous of these our own times, such as that degenerate fraud Aleister Crowley.

Herodotus' *Histories* is the source for the legendary wealth of Croesus of Lydia.

> When the Castel Sismondo was adequately complete, a masque was held. Domenico of Piacenza came to Rimini from Ferrara and d'Este. We danced in the great court, some seventy-five ladies and eighty-seven gentlemen of the town. Several of the gentlemen at any time would play upon the lute and viol, the sweet flute, and the *piffero* and *piva,* changing with the dances. We danced *carole*, the round dances *ride* and *ballonchii*, and *frottole* I would note Polissena, who moved with practised form, but with a stiffness born of joylessness. For my part, I was at first afraid that my lack of courtly learning would be apparent, but many there who were older than me had not learned to dance while young; I was, next to these, the embodiment of grace. In the *basse danse* I partnered Sigismondo, by his choice. He had danced with many other girls and women, so this was not of note. But to me, Cardinal Bessarion, it was as though Phoebus courted Terpsichore as her sisters stood by forgotten. We continued into a *rondo*, spinning and whirling with the singers and the thymes. I thought at that moment that I would believe only in a god who knows how to dance. Sigismondo moved his head forwards beside mine and whispered into my ear "if I wear clothes heavy with inlaid gold, emit soft Syrian scents, my hair combed by the hand of an artisan, a Phrygian cloak, hand-painted, falling from my shoulder, and if we perform artistic festive dances, or I put on my face new masks, I do all of this out of profound love, so that I may be pleasing to you, my dear girl."

Domenico of Piacenza was a famed dancing-master, ordinarily patronised by the d'Este court. The *piffero* was a woodwind instruments similar to the oboe, while the *piva* was a bagpipe of single drone and chanter. The various dances mentioned are all understood to be varieties of community dances, closer perhaps to the *cèilidh* than the modern ball. Isotta returns to her comparison of Sigismondo to Apollo, here referred to by his epithet 'Phoebus'. Terpsichore is the muse of dance.

> With no other hope in my life, I counted the one hundred and seventy long weeks between that day and the death of Polissena, when Sigismondo was free to court me. I know it to be a sin, to have rejoiced at her death; do you, I wonder, know what it is for a woman to love so, as the Lord decreed for us in punishment for the sin of Eve? He was the lord of my life: haughty and handsome, strong in mind and arm, patron to all the human arts, made of life and blood and passion, by which he loved me. Other women he had also. He was cruel, in love as in war. He would be villein to none; nor man, nor god, nor me.
>
> I shall make an end, Your Eminence, lest in recounting my errors my letter should become longer than all Boccaccio's tales of Prince Galeotto. I recant all my sins. Bless me, I beg you; pray for my soul.

Boccaccio's *Decameron* is subtitled 'The Tales of Prince Galeotto'. This is the same character as Galehaut in the Arthurian cycle as mentioned in the account of Ugo Tedeschini. Galeotto is both title and author of the book in which Francesca and Paulo Malatesta read of the illicit love of Guinevere and Lancelot which led to their fatal affair, as recounted in *Inferno*, Canto V. This is the final allusion given by Isotta in a letter heavy with the display of her learning in the Renaissance fashion. Her mentioning Dante and Boccaccio is almost required by her choice of literary Florentine rather than Latin.

Her several comparisons of Sigismondo to Apollo merely continue the parallels drawn by Bassinio da Parma in his *Hesperis* and literally set in stone in the *Tempio*. The various other classical allusions drawn include of course pagan Romans but Greek references and sources are also numerous, reflecting the Malatesta connections to the Greek east through the Morea as noted elsewhere. These of course take on a special relevance in a letter directed to Basilios Bessarion, who, in his yearning for the restoration of the empire of that Greek east, had caused the destruction of the love of Isotta's life. It may seem a terrible irony that this is the priest to whom Isotta sent her letter of repentant confession: I shall argue elsewhere that this contrition is illusory[1].

---

[1] See 'A Further Discovery'

Isotta continued to rule Rimini until 1474. Her authority was continually challenged by Sigismondo's other son Roberto: her death in 1474 was rumoured to have been a consequence of poisoning on the orders of Roberto, as indeed had probably been the case with Sallustio. Roberto then assumed rule of Rimini with the blessing of Pope Sixtus IV.

Figure 14: Medal of Sigismondo Malatesta by Matteo de' Pasti, drawing by A.B. Cromar

The Letter of Sophia Palaiologina,

The Letter of Sophia Palaiologina, Sister of Andreas Palaiologos, Despot of the Morea, to Cardinal Basilios Bessarion, July 1472

Sophia, who had been Zoe, was the second child of Thomas Palaiologos by Catherine Zaccaria. The date of her birth is unclear, but it would have been in the 1440s. Her family were in the Morea as Constantinople was taken, but she would still have been young in 1460 when the Hexamillion wall was breached and the Morea fell to the Sultan's forces. Along with her mother and siblings, she remained under Venetian protection in the fortress of Angelokastro on Corfu as her father went on to Rome seeking support and assistance.

Zoe's father died on the 12th of May 1465, and, together with her siblings, she was adopted by the Papacy. Her older sister Helena was married to Lazar Branković, Despot of Serbia. Andreas, the older of her two younger brothers, was, upon the death of their father, recognised in the west as rightful Despot of the Morea, and in time would additionally claim the title 'Emperor of Constantinople'.

Paul II was in office by this time, and he placed Bessarion in charge of Zoe's welfare. This was also when her name was changed at the Pope's suggestion. In my notes to Paul's letter I mention his attempts to arrange marriages for her, prior to Bessarion suggesting one to Ivan III, Grand Prince of Moscow.

In 1462, at the start of Prince Ivan's reign, his dominion was not large, and was one of several under the 'Tatar Yoke' of the Golden Horde. He campaigned against the neighbouring Novgorod Republic and the Grand Duchy of Lithuania. After his first wife died in 1467, Ivan was receptive to the Pope's proposal of a marriage to Sophia.

The arrangements took from early 1469 to 1472. As Paul insists in his letter, a first marriage ceremony was conducted in Rome, although Ivan was not present: he was represented by his ambassador, one Ivan Fryazin. This was on the 1st of June 1472: at the end of that month Sophia departed for Moscow, accompanied by Cardinal Bessarion.

The Greek in which Sophia Palaiologos has written this letter differs markedly from that used by her father in his, or indeed any other of her age. It is archaic, though imperfectly so, employing vocabulary, grammatical form and syntax from classical Attic and Ionic examples. It contains much post-classical vocabulary also, and a fair number of what can only reasonably be errors, in attempting to recreate a classical idiom. It is most reminiscent of the style of the *Alexiad* of Anna Komnena written three centuries earlier. Sophia's source for the literary idiom employed in her letter would not escape Bessarion: it is probable that Bessarion himself had provided Sophia with her copy of the *Alexiad*, and the parallels Sophia wished him to draw would have been clear.

As some slight indication of the royal associations of this style, but avoiding further artificial obscurantism in the English, I have presented Sophia Palaiologina as employing the first person plural, which I have then capitalised. Her letter being short, I give its translation in full:

> Sacrificed to the necessity of Our journey, your companionship is sorely missed, dear Basilios. Our heart is filled with anguish at the news of your ill health, and that this has prevented you from escorting Us further towards Moscow. While We shall miss your cultured company, the journey before Us will be onerous, and it is a comfort to Us at least to know that you will be spared this hardship and inconvenience. We believe that We shall not meet with you again in this world, and so leave for you this letter, by means of which to bid you farewell, and to give to you Our thanks, however inadequate they may be, for your lifetime of faithful service to Our family.
>
> We remember the great efforts you have made on Our behalf, in securing Our passage from the Morea to Rome by way of Corfu, to keep Our person from the hands of the Turk. We thank you for what We know to have been your most noble intentions in Our regard.
>
> We must make to you now a declaration which We know will cause you distress. You should be aware that knowing the pain which it will cause to you likewise causes an equal pain in Us. In time the matter will become known, however, and it were, We feel, better and more fitting to the

honourable esteem in which We hold you, that We announce it to you first, and in the privacy of this letter.

We shall go to be wed to Ivan, King of the Russians, and be his queen, far from Rome, and far from the glory that was Constantinople, the second Rome. We shall go to dwell in the dark and the cold at the far limits of the world. We assent to this marriage which you have arranged for Us, as you know well.

We go as a princess of the house of Palaiologos. We shall bring the light of civilisation to the dark winters of the Rus. We carry within Us the bloodline of the Emperors of the Romans. We go to found a third Rome, that the Empire shall rise again in the north; and that Empire will be, Cardinal Bessarion, of the Church of the Empire, established by Theodosius as Emperor, of the Orthodoxy agreed by the Council of the Church at Nicaea nearly eleven centuries now past. We repudiate the Latin Church and We deny the claims of the Bishop of Rome. We know you to be a learned man, a great scholar, but we cannot agree with you to compromise Our faith with the Western Catholics. We shall not, moreover, ask Our husband, nor the Russian people, to abandon the true and Orthodox Church for the Latin Rite, that they might gain the favour of the western Princes at the cost of their immortal souls. We are a daughter of Caesars, born in the purple, and We shall be mother to Caesars, to bring the peoples of the world again into the protection of the Empire under the one true and Orthodox faith.

We know that this news will bring you pain, dear Basilios, but We hope that you will repent your pragmatism of union with the Latins and return to the mother church before you depart this life. You are dear to Us, and while We are aware that Our choice in this is contrary to what you had intended, We hope that you will see that We are unable to do otherwise, and We hope, moreover, that you return to the true faith before the Lord takes you from this life. You are in Ravenna: go, perhaps, to the Basilica there dedicated to Saint Vitalis, and see the presbytery with its mosaics, such as were in the Holy Wisdom: of Christ and the Saints, but also Justinian and Theodora, Emperor and Empress, just as in

> the audience chamber of the Imperial Palace, richer and more heavenly than the poor frescos of the west. Remember the true faith. We do not choose the cup which is placed before Us, but We shall drink from it all the same, and render thereby that which is the due both of Caesar and of God.

In 988 Vladimir Prince of Kiev and the Kievan Rus, had converted to Orthodox Christianity and married Anna, sister of Byzantine Emperor Basil II, and then in 1325 the seat of the Metropolitan Bishop of the Kievan church moved to Moscow. Now, a century and a half later, like Vladimir before him, Ivan was able to marry a Byzantine Imperial Princess; unlike Vladimir, Ivan was able to claim that Sophia brought with her the succession to the Imperial throne. She introduced to Moscow all the grandeur and etiquette of the Imperial Court of Constantinople, under the symbol of the double-headed eagle and everything it represented. Ivan went on to conquer Novgorod, throw off the Tatar Yoke, and greatly expand his territory. He styled himself 'Tsar', which is to say 'Caesar'. His son Vasily III and his grandson Ivan IV continued the territorial expansion to a scale which was undeniably imperial: Ivan IV was the first to style himself 'Tsar of all Rus'. Today he is more usually known as Ivan the Terrible.

Bessarion fell ill before leaving Italy, staying in Ravenna. He was not a young man, being almost seventy years of age. Sophia appears to have sent him this letter as she continued her journey northward to Moscow. It is known from other sources that her return to Orthodoxy was clear even before reaching Russia: here she appears genuinely to have wanted to tell Bessarion herself rather than have him learn it from other sources. It is likely that Sophia's expressions of concern and compassion for him are genuine, despite her clearly being aware that he has attempted to use her for his political ends: Bessarion had been, after all, the best friend her family had following the fall of the Morea, and had been a father figure to her since she had been in Italy. That he should have had a hand in arranging her marriage would hardly have been inappropriate. Legend has it that part of Sophia's dowry were books provided by Bessarion which went on to become the basis of the famed library of Ivan the Terrible.

With her rejection of Catholicism Sophia thwarted Bessarion's plans to bring the Russians into the sphere of influence of the Papacy. Was Bessarion brought back to the Mother Church of Orthodoxy as Sophia urged? To what degree the news contributed to Bessarion's decline we cannot know, but he did not recover, dying in Ravenna on the 18th of November 1472.

The route north from Ravenna followed by Sophia took her through the German lands. Two years ago now a sealed train left Zurich to pass through wartime Germany towards her enemy's capital of Moscow: as Sophia Palaiologina had once travelled to found the Tsarist Empire of Russia, Vladimir Ilyich Lenin went to oversee its end.

The last letter of the collection is finished, and Cardinal Basilios Bessarion is dead. This his final scheme came to nothing: in the words of Ecclesiastes "then I looked on all the works that my hands had wrought, and on the labour that I had laboured to do: and behold, all was vanity and vexation of spirit, and there was no profit under the sun."

The mosaics of Ravenna remain to this day, created with the establishment of the Exarchate upon the re-conquest of western territories by the Emperor Justinian. In the apse of the Basilica of San Vitale, taking their place alongside the patriarchs of the Old Testament, the representatives of the twelve tribes of Israel, the four evangelists and the lamb of God, are the images of Emperor Justinian and Empress Theodora. Both are clad in Tyrian purple. Halos encircle their heads against that gold of heaven gifting their images an otherworldliness which has, in our times, so inspired the Viennese painter Gustav Klimt. Each is flanked by the senior members of their court. The frescoes of the Italian baroque which adorn the high dome of that church are poor things by comparison, more tired and faded by a mere two centuries than the Imperial couple after many times that duration. Justinian's reconquest of the west lasted rather less well than his golden-splendored image: the Exarchate of Ravenna came to an end in the eighth century, conquered first by Lombards, then by Franks, and then the Papacy.

Did Bessarion go to the Basilica before he died? And what thoughts, what feelings stirred the heart of the sick old man, if he indeed stood before that Orthodox vision of golden heaven, abode of God, destination of the blessed?

Our word 'heaven' is from Old English '*heofan*', which is simply the sky. Dante - that other exile who had died in Ravenna - used the word '*paradiso*', the etymology of which goes back to ancient middle eastern enclosed gardens, with all the associations of luxuriant felicity given to these by desert peoples; Eden is merely their primordial epitome. These two senses become confused and conflated: in translation 'heaven' is often used for Dante's '*ciel*' (modern Italian '*cielo*', simply the sky); 'paradise' may be used to distinguish the place of bliss from the prosaic matter of altitude.

We have already noted Bessarion's contribution, by way of his insistence on a mathematically competent commentary to the *Almagest,* towards the challenge to the Ptolemaic cosmos by Nicholas Copernicus. This contradicted scripture, of which several psalms and verses assert that" the world is firmly established; it cannot be moved". In the following century Giordano Bruno would propose that stars were distant suns, perhaps possessed of their own planets. He was burned at the stake in 1600. 33 years later Galileo Galilei would survive his inquisition through recantation of heliocentrism, despite the attributed "*eppur si muove*".

Poggio Bracciolini's use of lenses, in the form of his eyeglasses, and Leon Battista Alberti's comments on the improved mirrors of Murano, constitute the technological advances in optics which, alongside Alhazen's theories as adopted by Alberti, allowed Galileo to construct telescopes, and so more closely inspect the heavens. He was able to conclude that Jupiter was orbited by at least four moons, and his discovery of the phases of Venus rendered the Ptolemaic model untenable.

Neither the distances nor the sizes of the background stars were apparent to Galileo: he believed that their imperceptible parallaxes were due to the limitations of his optical technology. Developments after him expanded the scale of the cosmos beyond the empyrean which Archimedes could fill with counted grains of sand, towards Cusanus' boundless infinite. The earth could no longer be claimed as central, nor was the abode of God apparent in these observations. Isaac Newton automated this new order through universal gravity, allowing Laplace to dispense with God as a hypothesis, and Nietzsche to now pronounce Him dead. Was it to man's advantage to have cast out his creator and stand alone beneath the greater majesty of uncreated sky, an infinite vacuum unstained by purpose, life, or love?

Figure 15: Imperial crest of the Palaiologoi, drawing by A.B. Cromar

A Further Discovery,

Epilogue to the Letter of Isotta degli Atti

The letter written by Isotta Malatesta degli Atti to Cardinal Basilios Bessarion is singular in a number of respects. It is my proposal that these peculiarities may be explained by postulating the presence within her letter of a second message in addition to its superficially apparent content, this being quite contrary in tone to that of the letter itself, and concealed both ingeniously and artfully.

As evidence in support of this contention, the first point of note is that the language in which the letter is written is not the Romagnol which would have been Lady Isotta's native dialect, but rather a version of Tuscan: specifically the literary Florentine of Dante, Boccaccio, and Petrarch. The Florentine is somewhat imperfectly employed, as might be expected of a less than fluent author, accustomed perhaps to reading the language, but unfamiliar with it for the purposes of composition. This choice must in no wise be conceived as a courtesy extended to Cardinal Bessarion, for although a man of such learning as he was should have comprehended it quite ably, the Cardinal would, of course, have had Greek for his native tongue, and Latin as a priest of the Roman Church. The explanation must be sought elsewhere.

It is to be observed that the letter of Lady Isotta includes some dozen numbers distributed throughout the text, often in a manner which is clearly forced. Specifically these are: a *dozen dozen* nights (144); *all the years of Ishmael* (137); the sun which numbers *all the year's days* (365); *three hundred and forty* days remaining to this year; *three hundred and thirty* verses into Dante's journey (the *sospiri, pianti e alti guai* occur, in fact, 31 lines earlier); Sigismondo staying at the Atti family home *all the weeks of one year* (52); the number of the cards of the *Tarocco Bolognese (62);* the number of [Bessarion's] years (67); *seventy-five* ladies and *eighty-seven* gentlemen attending Sigismondo's masque; the *one hundred and seventy* weeks until the death of Polissena; and *all Boccaccio's tales of Prince Galeotto* (100). It is my contention that these numbers represent a form of book cipher, or more precisely a book code, for which the required code book is the letter itself. The procedure is thus: for each number in turn, the word corresponding to that number is identified, as counted from the start of the letter;

from that point are then read the eleven consecutive syllables of a hendecasyllabic line. Additionally I claim that in two cases - namely fifty-two and sixty-two - two consecutive lines are to be read. These come from the second paragraph of the letter, precisely that section where the unnatural style is most conspicuous.

The fourteen such lines thus reconstructed comprise a sonnet after Petrarch, so:

Est'uovo, Bessario, Cardinale
Ti offro, la mi' anima umana,
Così che tu la rompa, sbucci, legga,
In segn' ignoti scritto, confessione,
l'inchiostro del aceto e alume,
Che non da te imploro la clemenza
O Dio altro, mio Malatesta
Dannato all'inferno, certamente;
Anzi con lui restare là in basso
affreterò, com'un' altra Francesca
Con suo miglio Paulo, o Orfeo
Per sempre con Euridice, un uomo
della rafinatezza e ricchezza,
Adorerò, il mio proprio Cristo.

It will perhaps be argued that this conjecture is rather improbable. Set against this are the following observations: the first is, bluntly, that it works, in that a comprehensible sonnet is indeed generated; furthermore the choice of the Florentine language, and the idiom of its employment, is otherwise rather queer; then, too, the inclusion of the numbers is awkward and unnatural; finally the mention by Isotta of her discussing cryptography with Leon Battista Alberti is otherwise an inexplicably odd aside. The same may be said of the mention of hendecasyllabic verse: incorrect for the Greek to which Isotta appears to allude in her letter, but, indeed, the metre of the Petrarchan sonnet. Taken as a piece these constitute a series of clues leading towards a message which, while hidden, is clearly intended to be discovered.

The result might be deemed clumsy, or even artless, when assessed as a sonnet compared against the Petrarchan ideal, or other artists of the time. Such a judgement should properly be weighed against the feat of its secretion within the letter by a technique, so far as we are aware, of Lady Isotta's own devising. For a woman of the fifteenth century, with the education available to her as such, to have conceived of this, much less executed it, approaches the unimaginable, attesting to a rare and impressive mind.

I propose the following translation into English, although having even less claim to aesthetic worth than the original of Lady Isotta. Note that, contrary to common English practice, one must here assume the Greek pronunciation of Euridice with a hard 'c' and a pronounced final vowel in order to rhyme with 'eternity':

> This little egg, this human soul of mine,
> I offer, Cardinal Bessarion,
> That you might crack, and shell, and read thereon
> My true confession, writ in secret sign,
> By ink of alum drowned in sour wine,
> That I, my husband Malatesta gone
> To hell, undoubtedly, fall not upon
> My knees beseeching mercy, God's or thine:
> Instead to him most gladly shall I haste,
> That Orpheus shall with his Eurydice
> Remain in hell, and know that it sufficed,
> Francesca to my man of wealth and taste,
> My better Paulo, for eternity,
> To worship this, my own, my personal Christ.

So it appears that Isotta Malatesta degli Atti, inspired, we may imagine, by techniques discussed many years before with Leon Battista Alberti, secreted within her contrite, repentant and God-fearing letter to Cardinal Basilios Bessarion her real message, unrepentant, defiant of both men and God, conveyed in a humanist vernacular after the *dolce stil novo.*

Did Isotta genuinely expect to find herself in hell with Sigismondo after death? And to what degree would she further expect that damnation to accord with that described by Dante for their precursors, Paulo and Francesca? Her use of literary Florentine fits both that comparison and also her chosen sonnet form: she is clearly playing a literary game. It may be that Isotta and Sigismondo were both Epicurean in their belief of the death of the soul with the body, but this would seem not to accord with the construction of the *Tempio Malatestiano* as their shared, grandiose tomb. They perhaps deemed this memorial the only afterlife worthy of concern, in the fashion of the pagans. I think this is unlikely though: even if they had chosen to live and die on terms of their own, shunning the Christian offer of Heaven, this is still fundamentally different from the resignation of the shades of the dead in Virgil or Homer, for whom no other end was conceivable: the damned of Dante's *Inferno* are aware that Heaven exists and is denied to them.

The impact of Dante's *Commedia* has been mainly felt in terms of his depiction of hell, rather than purgatory or heaven: one suspects that there are more people today who have heard the phrase "Dante's Inferno", and understand this to be an account of a journey through the circles of hell, than could connect his name with the phrase "The Divine Comedy" or even venture a description of what that indeterminate entity might be. I further propose that Dante has thereby been largely responsible for the prevailing modern conception of the underworld. The tradition goes back to Odysseus and then Aeneas, but the vision of a place of damnation and punishment derives from Dante's work. In the English-speaking world at least, Milton's *Paradise Lost* partially updated and partially reinforced Dante's conception, but the debt Milton owes to Dante is obvious. Of course the adopted perspectives differ fundamentally: Dante puts himself as a character in a work populated by familiar human personalities from his own time and back through history, Virgil selected as his guide explicitly to present Dante and his work as heir to Virgil's poetic greatness; Milton instead focusses on that epitome of all antiheroes in the person of Satan.

I have myself had reason to confront the impact of Dante's vision on our collective psyche. Walking alone into the Cairngorms one April, making for remote, deep-set Loch Avon, I miscalculated the conditions I would encounter: while familiar enough with that environment to know that it would still be winter there, I had not reckoned with quite the volume of recent snowfall which met me. Persistent cloud then reduced visibility to a few yards' thick light of total white-out. I pressed on, either fighting through chest-deep drifts between the boulders of the steeper slopes, or falling through feeble, snow-disguised ice to soak to my knees in the ponds and streams hidden beneath any flatter surface. By the time I had waded down to the shores of Loch Avon, I could not initially tell whether the few yards of water visible before me were truly the loch or just another pool. I stopped, listened, confirming this to be the loch only by the sound, extending away from me through the fog and murky air, of water softly lapping the shore.

An awful existential horror struck me at that moment. The remote solitude, the oppressive gloom, the requirement for continual, Sisyphean effort - if I let my purpose cool then so would I, to freeze in sweated clothing - and the sickly lifelessness of this shrunken, achromatic world defiled me with a flood of loneliness like I have never otherwise known. I felt with absolute clarity that I had walked to the shore of Acheron through the dun smoke of Hell. I also considered, incongruously, that this mental connection of what was, in truth, a perfectly natural scene to the notion of Hell followed from the lasting cultural impact of Dante: his vision differed in the key respect of at least not being so appallingly lonely.

If Dante's work could still so impress itself upon me after all these centuries, how much more must its impact have been on Isotta degli Atti, so much closer in time and space to its creation? Whether this means we should interpret her sonnet as indicating her genuine beliefs about the afterlife, or rather demonstrating the degree to which such ideas were literary conventions, I confess myself wholly unable to decide.

In any event, it appears that in the end Cardinal Basilios Bessarion was undone. His schemes for the relief of Constantinople had amounted to little, at the cost of the contrived damnation of a human soul. Half a century previously he had been a priest of a church which he had since abandoned in order to save an empire on which the sun had now forever set. He had been a pupil of Georgios Gemistus Pletho, who, though professing no Christianity, had turned the other cheek to the catastrophe of Byzantium, fixing his mind's eye on the eternal spiritual. All that remained of Pletho to this world lay in a sarcophagus displayed on the flank of a temple which was no longer a church, a trophy claimed in pagan triumph by that Sigismondo Malatesta who Bessarion's worldly ambitions had seen damned. Malatesta thus displayed to Bessarion his identification of Pletho's absolute intellectual integrity with Sigismondo's own defiance, contrasted with Bessarion's futile compromise. At the end Sophia, who had been the girl Zoe, placed in Bessarion's charge, even she had defied him. Did he recognise by then that Isotta, too, had, for love, joined her husband in his perdition and contempt? As with so many questions raised by these documents, we simply cannot know.

Figure 16: Dante shows to Aeneas Piccolomini the shades of Isotta and Sigismondo Malatesta in Hell, after the episode of Francesca and Paulo Malatesta from *Inferno* Canto V, drawing by A.B. Cromar

Appendix: Notes of George Lewis Quain

We live, once more, in interesting times. Populist demagogues stir up a swell of nationalism. A dogma is abroad of the existential threat posed to western civilisation by Islamic incursion, or by a tide of refugees across the Mediterranean. The unreason of 'fake news' undermines trust in the established media, a development one might regard as progress except that it questions also the existence in the world of such things as science, or expertise. That is the untarmacadamed road back to benighted savagery.

I mention the above by way of full disclosure, attempting to recognise what biases I may carry into my reading of these documents of Dr. Alexander Blaikie Cromar. I have, in addition, come to think of him as a friend, despite the not inconsiderable inconvenience to that relationship of his having died one hundred years ago this month. It is to this centenary I owe my possession of these his writings, for it provided the impetus for a descendant of his to gift them to me. This source, who wishes to remain anonymous, had inherited the documents without any associated use for, or interest in them. They further confessed that nobody in the family seemed to have any idea of the whereabouts of the original letters which the Doctor claims to have bought at the emporium of *Atti e Figli* in Bologna in 1910, or even whether those letters had ever actually existed.

What *is* known of Alexander Blaikie Cromar may be summarised as follows. He was descended on his father's side from farming stock, his paternal grandparents having left the eastern lee of the Grampian Mountains in the early nineteenth century and moved to Aberdeen. His father, Donald Cromar, grew up to be a merchant in the city, one sufficiently successful that in 1848 he married one Mary Blaikie, a daughter of that family of wealthy industrialists who provided the city with two of her Lord Provosts at around this time. This prestige led to the Blaikie surname being retained in double-barreled form for the couple's children, of whom the first was Alexander, born in 1850. After attending Robert Gordon's School, Alexander was amongst the first to train in the new medical faculty of Aberdeen University, itself recently formed by the merger of the ancient King's and Marischal

Colleges. His professional life as a physician continued from 1875 until his retirement in 1910.

It is not, however, his medical career, but rather Dr. Cromar's amateur passions which interest us here. He was what might best be termed an antiquarian, with interests ranging broadly across archaeology, ancient and medieval art, history, language and literature. Although in his day 'amateur' had not yet been loaded with negative connotations by the business-fetishist world we endure today, the time when such generalists might achieve significant mastery in any area had already passed, and Alexander was not a man of independent means in the manner of the celebrated amateurs who had preceded him.

The amateur, though, is driven neither by fame, nor by gain, but by love alone. Throughout his working life Alexander pursued his extracurricular studies. His schooling had included, by modern standards, a significant classical component, providing a grounding in both Latin and Greek. His *Alma Mater* continued to provide access to scholarship. He was involved with, though never a fellow of, the Society of Antiquaries of Scotland. He was in any event expected, as a member of the professional middle classes, to cultivate an interest in the arts.

It might be imagined that a fascination with the past would render his tastes conservative, but his work in medicine required him to keep abreast of the latest advances at a time of tremendous progress. It seems that he also saw more acutely than many, even to our own day, the implications of Darwin's theory, not only in its challenge to religious dogma, but also, by way of Freud and others, that our belief in our rationality is a delusion.

As a consequence, in the arts his preference seems to have been for the contemporary. One of his drawings which accompanied these writings is of Danaë, derived from the painting by Gustav Klimt of 1907. It seems that he saw the original when he visited Vienna on his way to Italy in 1910, arriving from Paris on the Orient Express, before making for Venice. Quite what his Presbyterian neighbours back in Ferryhill would have made of that image is difficult to imagine.

On the 28th of June 1914 Otto von Bismarck's prediction of "some damn foolish thing in the Balkans" came to pass with Gavrilo

Princip's assassination of Archduke Franz Ferdinand, dragging all Europe and the world beyond into the Great War. David Cromar, oldest son of Alexander and Margaret, joined the Gordon Highlanders, rising to the rank of Major before being killed in the Spring Offensive of 1918. My hypothesis is that Doctor Cromar reacted to his grief at that loss, to all his horror at the war, in these documents: that, at the same time as in Trieste and then Zürich James Joyce was writing *Ulysses*, in Aberdeen Alexander Blaikie Cromar was attempting a similarly experimental Modernist work of literature. In it he had intended to address the trauma he suffered at what he saw as the end of European civilisation as he knew it.

I do Dr. Cromar the courtesy of dismissing the possibility that he would attempt to pass off as genuine a crude historical hoax. This is in spite of the observation that such investigations as I have carried out suggest that the alleged content of the collection of letters does not contradict what is otherwise historically established in any decisive way. Minor peculiarities could reasonably be deemed merely a consequence of Dr. Cromar's amateur translations: one wonders what Latin of Malatesta Novello would become the idiomatically English "as well to be hanged for a sheep as a lamb", for example. Even the reconstruction of the sonnet of Isotta degli Atti is technically plausible from the information we have at our disposal, if due account is taken of the lower number of words in the equivalent Italian. Florentine, *sensu stricto.*

However, it will presumably be agreed that here we sorely test the elastic of credibility. Dr. Cromar himself admits that it "approaches the unimaginable". What are the consequences if it reaches it? Is there another way, where the letters indeed existed nowhere outside of the mind of Dr. Alexander Blaikie Cromar, but neither are these his documents intended seriously to persuade us otherwise? A somewhat sophisticated hoax, perhaps?

My next move is further to assume that his intention was not to comment upon the world of *quattrocento* Italy, but instead to address issues of his own time and place, albeit obliquely and allegorically. Admittedly what follows may be sufficiently complex to render the hypothesis of Isotta degli Atti's secretion of her sonnet appear more plausible by comparison. I appeal to the reader for both patience and tolerance. Indeed, I will argue that this complexity was a necessary aspect of Doctor Cromar's conception.

I propose that he was building his creation on a foundation of counterfeit fifteenth century Italian letters because there he saw the birthplace of his own culture. As Petrarch had looked back to the example of classical Rome across what he saw as the dark ages which had followed it, so Doctor Cromar saw the Renaissance to which Petrarch had contributed as the beginning of an enlightened age which was now ending in the darkness of world war.

We have seen that Sigismondo Malatesta claimed descent from the patrician Scipios of classical Rome, that his image might be illuminated by their glory. In this he was merely in keeping with the spirit of his age and country: the humanists such as Petrarch and Poggio Bracciolini looked to Cicero or Lucretius in an equivalent fashion. But such conjuring of the ancient spirit of Rome was a practice hardly limited to *quattrocento* Italians. It was that impulse which had brought Charlemagne to Rome to be crowned Holy Roman Emperor by Pope Leo III on Christmas Day of 800 AD. From him to where had this lineage passed? To France and to the Holy Roman Empire, which by Dr. Cromar's day had begot a Germany ruled by a Caesar - Kaiser Wilhelm II - and an Austro-Hungarian Empire under Kaiser Franz Joseph. Surely, though, Constantine the Great had taken the seat of empire to Byzantium five centuries before Charlemagne, making the Palaiologoi the true successors of Rome? And so had not Sophia brought that lineage to the Caesars of Tzarist Moscow? Or had Mehmet II by conquest made himself *Qayser-i Rûm* - Caesar of the Romans - as he claimed? When Franz Joseph's nephew was shot these were the various powers who proceeded to tear each other and all Europe apart.

At the same time as Dr. Cromar was writing, on the opposing shore of the awful chasm which had sundered Europe, Oswald Spengler was completing *Der Untergang des Abendlandes* - 'The Decline of the West'. In it Spengler argued that, in place of a linear, teleological and Eurocentric progress from savagery to civilisation, history was more accurately characterised as the emergence of a number of independent cultures, to be regarded as super-organisms with a finite lifespan. Once these mature into civilisations, their youthful energy expended, they necessarily decay and pass away, Spengler claimed. While of course a German perspective would have its differences from that of the Aberdonian, did these two men, whose instincts were not those of narrow nationalism, possess an essentially similar sense of the *zeitgeist*?

Spengler's prediction was of a long deterioration of western culture, rationalism and democracy gradually failing, to be abandoned. The only bulwark against fully chaotic anarchy remaining at this point is "Caesarism" in which Spengler foresaw autocratic and extraconstitutional omnipotence of the central governmental executive, underpinned by populist appeals to nationalism. He viewed Benito Mussolini as his first ideal of this, and he always retained a personal distaste for the crude racialism of German National Socialism. His prediction was that the struggle with democracy would continue until around the turn of the millennium, at which time the final victory of despotism would occur.

Oswald Spengler's work, however, was one of philosophy and historiography. He had a big idea about how history operated which he proceeded to describe. The irony here is that this very tendency towards a universal, mechanistic explanation of how the world works is the signature behaviour of Spengler's own particular civilisation. His own argument portrayed this civilisation as only one among many. If his idea was correct, it would at the same time necessarily be the product of his own culture's arbitrary paradigm. I propose that this paradox provides the key to understanding Doctor Cromar's alternative approach.

Consider the movements current in the art world when Dr. Cromar was conceiving of his work. Cubism challenged the convention of depicting objects within a painting from a single viewpoint. The rules of this convention were precisely those set down by Leon Battista Alberti in *Da Pittura.* Moreover, essentially the same challenge, Cromar realised, had already been made in Alberti's time by Nicholas of Cusa in discussing the monks of the Benedictine Abbey of Tegernsee contemplating a true icon. Marcel Duchamp's 1912 painting 'Nude Descending A Staircase No.2' added multiple perspectives of an object in time as well as in space. Given this example from the world of painting, I contend that Alexander Blaikie Cromar contrived a literary form which provided him with an equivalent variety of perspectives. By this means he hoped to escape the trap of the single dogmatic point of view into which Oswald Spengler had fallen.

Through Nicholas of Cusa's critique, Doctor Cromar presents Leon Battista Alberti's rules of perspective as having led to a world view which begot modern science. Alberti's grid and visual pyramid become the Cartesian co-ordinates within which Newton's laws of motion can operate, thence the Enlightenment and the industrial world of the nineteenth century. Of course if he was to avoid the trap of Spengler's single explanation, Doctor Cromar could not insist too much upon this account of the rise of modernity. So he hinted also at the proclamation of the atheistic atomism of Epicureanism in Poggio Bracciolini's rediscovery of Lucretius' *De Rerum Natura*. While the challenge to religious orthodoxy inherent in that philosophy was more apparent than in Alberti's perspective, and so more vigorously opposed, by the nineteenth century science had accepted an explanation of chemistry essentially in agreement with it. This was, though, an atomism with no place for the unpredictability of Lucretian *clinamen*, but one which fitted into the deterministic, clockwork mechanism of the Newtonian universe.

Dr. Cromar's notes to the second letter of Nicholas of Cusa also mention Albert Einstein, whose four papers of his 1905 *annus mirabilis* undermined the accepted certainties of both these scientific dogmas. By the time of Dr. Cromar's death the full implications of Einstein's paper on the Photoelectric Effect, these being the lack of determinism at the atomic scale inherent in quantum mechanics, which corresponds to Lucretius' *clinamen,* were yet to become fully clear. However, the absence of a rigid and objective frame of reference for the macroscopic geometry of the world was fundamental to Einstein's paper on Special Relativity. As the artistic tradition gave way to multiple and shifting viewpoints, so the objective and deterministic scientific framework which had followed from Alberti's artistic viewpoint was shattered.

Nicholas of Cusa mentions the hubris of those who might "find some lands as yet unknown to Christendom out there beyond the sunset": by this means Doctor Cromar refers anachronistically to Columbus' voyage a generation after Cusa's death and the subsequent colonisation of the Americas. In 1903 is was the Americans Orville and Wilbur Wright who used internal combustion engine power "to fly up to the heavens as though to mock the angels". Perhaps Dr. Cromar foresaw that, if anyone could, it would be men of that nation who would "set their foot upon the moon".

Such a hypothesis in no way undermines Dr. Cromar's reading of Nicholas of Cusa referencing Lucian's *True Story* in those words, as this provides the ludic irony of anachronistic reflection necessary to Cromar's purpose.

And so we have Leon Battista Alberti as the midwife of the epoch of which Alexander Blaikie Cromar is the priest who administers extreme unction. Nicholas of Cusa is the prophetic voice foreseeing its course and demise. Poggio Bracciolini is included to lay the scene of the Renaissance world in which Dr. Cromar's characters act and speak. He has also a place of honour for his rediscovery of Lucretius' fateful work. The various other authors provide alternative perspectives on this world, including, finally, two women who both, in different ways, reject the roles men attempt to force upon them: may we here perhaps read a sympathy in Dr. Cromar for the suffragettes of his own day?

Of course there are contrary viewpoints, which is Cromar's point. George of Trebizond is a solitary, apocalyptic voice warning of the approaching end of the world, trying, as he sees it, to speak truth to power. He has misjudged that power, and the currents of history. History has painted him as a lunatic in consequence. There are Thomas Palaiologos and Basilios Bessarion, who both see their age as the end, after over two millennia, of the supreme polity, the greatest civilisation the world has ever known. And there is Sophia Palaiologina, who has determined that it will not end: she will effect a different *renaissance* all of her own.

Is it mere coincidence that Edward Hutton had, in 1906, published his historical novel *Sigismondo Pandolfo Malatesta, Lord of Rimini,* bringing the man and his legend more clearly into the public consciousness? For Dr. Cromar, Sigismondo Pandolfo Malatesta is the central figure around which these other characters orbit because he represents a third strand, after Alberti's geometry and Lucretius' Epicureanism, of explanation for the beginning of the modern world in the Italian Renaissance. This is his individualism, with its substantial relationship to Renaissance humanism. Sigismondo, in his self-fashioning promotion of his own image, in his refusal to submit to military or religious force, is made by Dr. Cromar into the *Übermensch* of Friedrich Nietzsche, for whom God is dead, and who must create his own morality. This is the same appeal which saw Sigismondo Malatesta's inclusion in the first 'Cantos' published in

1925 by that unrepentant fascist Ezra Pound. The great lie of that creed is the mythic championing of the human spirit by an inhuman, totalitarian political reality.

In Cromar's work Sigismondo does not speak of his own accord, but is viewed from the several perspectives of the authors of the letters. For Cusanus he embodies what he attempts to warn Bessarion about, which is where Alberti's ideas will ultimately lead. Sigismondo is respected for his martial competence by some, derided as a coward bereft of honour or shame by others. He is loved by Isotta for his independence of mind and nobility of spirit, which she sees as rising above the hypocrisy of the political intrigues of his day. He shows himself not to be the mere brute Pius painted him, recovering the bones of Gemistus Pletho from the Peloponnese because of his "love of learned men".

Malatesta here parodies the Christian practice of venerating the remains of Saints as relics, placing the bones of a confessed pagan on the side of the church which he has rebuilt as a temple dedicated to his own splendour. Georgios Gemistus Pletho cannot reasonably be described as a character in Dr. Cromar's creation, being dead before the date of Poggio Bracciolini's first letter. Instead he is a symbol. This symbol, from Poggio's recollection of him at the Council of Florence, is of the ideal philosopher, set disinterestedly apart from mundane or worldly concerns. As such he is contrasted with his former pupil Bessarion, whose political scheming is presented as motivating the whole collection of documents, and who, in Sophia Palaiologina's accusation, has sold his soul. The futility of his having done so is admonished by Sigismondo Malatesta, whom Bessarion had thought his pawn, through the placement of Pletho's bones in a place of renown on the *Tempio Malatestiano*. And so Bessarion, high priest and scholar, patron, political manipulator and warmonger, can be mocked at the end by a woman clinging to scraps of power, Isotta Malatesta degli Atti, even as she anticipates her own apparently inevitable murder.

It appears that, had he lived, Alexander Blaikie Cromar intended to build upon the framework of these letters his own literary reaction to the descent of European civilisation into the horror of the Great War. We cannot know what else he may have included, claimed, or predicted. His chosen literary form was clearly fundamentally different from the scholarly thesis in which Oswald Spengler reached an apparently similar conclusion. Both men foresaw the decline of western civilisation, from a phase of confidence in reason into one in which the limit of such confidence is reached, rationality is abandoned, and all is threatened with destruction and chaos. Spengler, who recognised in Mussolini the type of 'Caesar' who would take autocratic political control, predicted that this would be contested ground for some time, but that the trend would inevitably be away from faith in science, away from previously accepted facts, away from democracy, with the arts degenerating, towards a centuries-long twilight of western culture under populist tyrannies. Alexander Blaikie Cromar did not live to make explicit any such predictions, but, from what we have of his writings, it appears he shared Spengler's pessimistic view that he had lived to see at least the beginning of the end of the age: an age whose birth and nature he had, in his grief at its demise, explored in these documents purporting to be the lost letters of Cardinal Bessarion. The difference is that Cromar, stepping back from the brink of dogmatism, included Sophia Palaiologina and Isotta degli Atti's defiant insistence that their fates were their own to write.

There is an additional, tragic strand to Dr. Cromar's story, some shadows of which, I suggest, are cast across his text. I have published separately his 'A Letter for Maggie Cromar', written during a period of quarantine due to the 1918-1920 'Spanish Flu' pandemic. Within the same year of writing that letter and its accompanying poems to his wife, the disease returned and this time killed Alexander Blaikie Cromar in November of 1919. Naturally, he did not write his own death into his work. But some small hints are, I think, discernible of the contribution of his earlier experience of quarantine to his mood.

The '*Tre Corone*' of Florentine literature, Dante, Boccaccio and Petrarch, are woven throughout the various documents. His final flourish is to conjure a Petrarchan sonnet with a Dante-esque subject. But note that the last of Isotta's hidden numbers is one hundred, the number of "Boccaccio's tales of Prince Galeotto": the Decameron. While Boccaccio is not explicitly mentioned as often as Dante and Petrarch, in the most referenced scene of the *Commedia* it was Galeotto's account of Guinevere and Lancelot which led astray Francesca and Paulo Malatesta, from which Malatesta Novello draws parallels to the third Malatesta brother, Galeotto. I think it is not too much to suggest that there is a parallel being drawn between

Boccaccio's collection of tales, told in isolation from the pandemic of the Black Death, and Dr. Cromar's collection, written, at least in part, in isolation from the 'Spanish Flu'.

The foregoing is, as previously admitted, a complex argument for a peculiar hypothesis. I do not believe that this should be counted against it. Whatever interpretation the reader may wish to make of what they have read, it is difficult to conceive of a simple or trivial explanation. This, I claim, was central to Doctor Cromar's purpose: in a world descended into destruction, into crude tribalism, into savagery, or into enforced isolation in consequence of a pandemic, to insist upon the breadth and depth of culture, of the interconnections across the various aspects of human creativity, of the complexity and consequent richness of experience available to us as civilised human beings, becomes a posture of resistance, a gesture of defiance, and a revolutionary act.

From our vantage-point it is apparent that the age for which Doctor Cromar grieved was that of capitalism. Dr. Cromar argues that the Florentine Renaissance started when the Medici bank purchased mercenary military power to counter that of the landed warrior class with whom that power had traditionally resided in feudal medieval society. Capitalism would go on to harness art, science and all individual human creativity in the pursuit of commercial progress. It would be useless now to aspire to what Alexander Blaikie Cromar could attempt a century ago: the modernist conception was to repudiate post-Victorian values through the creation of something subversive, scandalous and generally antisocial; in the intervening time postmodernism, with its endemic irony and aesthetic populism, has rendered any such attempt futile, necessarily being received in late capitalist society with utter complacency.

Perhaps it makes little difference whether Dr Cromar invented these letters or translated them from older ones. He would have read the putative originals with his own eyes, a particular man of a particular time and place. Writing his translations would still have been a creative literary act. Linguistic choices always rest upon the enigma of how meaning finds its way into words through usage, so that the word cannot be divorced from its whole history of prior use. That Dr. Cromar's sentences bear the imprint of his own time tells us nothing of whether they are translations or originals, for in either case they are the product of a literary tradition as well as of real events.

The remains of Georgios Gemistus Pletho and Sigismondo Pandolfo Malatesta lie in their graves in the church in Rimini. The bones tell us that each was once a living human individual. The tombs testify that each was also something else, a character in a story, or many stories. Pletho became a supporting character in Sigismondo's story, as retold by Bassinio da Parma, by Matteo di Pasti, by Piero della Francesca. How much difference does it make whether the bones of Ugo Tedeschini lie somewhere in the soil of Emilia-Romagna? Whether once he truly spoke aloud in Romagnol his account of the *condottiere* Sigismondo Pandolfo Malatesta, before it was rewritten by Niccolò Perotti into Latin and rewritten again into English by Alexander Blaikie Cromar, or was invented by Perotti for some unknowable purpose, or only ever existed in the imagination of Dr. Cromar, his was in any case just one more history, one more story, one more perspective on Sigismondo Malatesta the man, with no more claim to a final truth than those of Pope Pius II or of Sigismondo himself. Any version would be only a reading, partaking in truth, but falling short of being fully true.

Ultimately, as with any history, any interpretation of the origin of the letters as written by Alexander Blaikie Cromar leaves us with documents which speak to us as much about the time in which he wrote them as the time of which they were written; both tell us as much about the writer as they do about their chosen subject. A story of the past may be made with a genuine attempt to determine the facts of what occurred, or it may also be made as an honest fiction: in either case the partiality remains. The irrevocable past has no use for history, which obtains meaning only as a mirror of the present.

George Lewis Quain

Aberdeen, November 2019